ONLY BY MISTAKE

ONLY BY MISTAKE

P. J. Kavanagh

JOHN CALDER · LONDON
RIVERRUN PRESS · NEW YORK

First published in 1986 by
John Calder (Publishers) Ltd
18 Brewer Street, London W1R 4AS
and in the United States of America in 1986 by
Riverrun Press Inc
1170 Broadway, New York, NY 10001

British Library Cataloguing in Publication Data

Kavanagh, P.J.
  Only by mistake.
  I. Title
  823'.914[F]   PR6061.A9

  ISBN 0-7145-4084-6
  ISBN 0-7145-4085-4 Pbk

Library of Congress Cataloging in Publication Data

Kavanagh, P.J. (Patrick Joseph) 1931
  Only By Mistake
  1. Title
  PR 6061 A 9054 1986   823'.914 86–4864

ISBN 0-7145-4084-6 (Riverrun Press)
ISBN 0-7145-4085-4 (Riverrun Press Paper)

Typeset in 11 on 12 point Baskerville by Alan Sutton Publishing Limited
Printed in Great Britain by Hillman Printers (Frome) Ltd, Somerset.

ONLY BY MISTAKE

1

The man who looked out of the window, between slightly parted curtains, was neither young nor old. He had placed the oil-lamp on the floor before he looked out, and his face lit from beneath had a pouchiness and jowliness about it. But when he picked up the lamp, after carefully closing the curtains, and the light fell full on him, the sags and marks on his face became less defined, almost unnoticeable; and his step back to his chair was youthful.

He put the lamp on a small table, picked up his book, and sat down.

Before opening the book, before leaning back in his chair, he listened.

Above the wind and the roaring of the sea he could just distinguish the sound of a car, or thought he did. But it did not grow louder, the engine noise, as it surely would have done if the car had turned down the valley. He strained to listen: no — nothing. There was only the sea, the wind, and the soft splutterings of peat in the grate. He let out his breath, lay back carefully in his chair, and opened the book:

'Think any number you like — double — add 12 to it — halve it — take away the original number — and there remains six.'

Well, there would, wouldn't there. He remembered the puzzle from his schooldays. Odd that Coleridge should begin his Notebook that way. But then, he didn't. It was guessed to be the beginning by his editor, two hundred years later.

Nevertheless, it was the right way to begin: inconsequentially, relaxed. Plan things too precisely and you paralyse yourself, go stiff, and bring the Fates down on

7

your back. . . . The man grunted, twitching his shoulders slightly, as though he felt the Fates descending.

He had certainly not thought this business through. Had just acted on impulse. He raised his head and listened again.

Had he covered his tracks well enough? There was sure to be something he'd forgotten. He settled his shoulders, frowned, and returned to his book, forcing it to lie open more flatly than it wished, so that its spine made a cracking noise:

'*Mem. — not to adulterise my time by absenting myself from my wife.*'

He stared into the fire. Coleridge enjoying himself with the word 'adulterise'. His had been a bad marriage, but not at this time, not yet. He thought of his own marriages and shut his eyes. These days, it occurred to him, his thoughts were like bare feet walking on gravel, they could go in no direction without hurting. That was precisely why he was reading Coleridge's *Notebooks* — to see if the private thoughts of another man could alter the course of his own.

Nevertheless. . . . *Had* the man on the mainland recognised him? In the dockside bar where he waited for the ferry the man had stared, as though he knew him. Dougal had turned away, not too quickly, his chin thrust deep into his black scarf and his tweed hat pulled down over his forehead. He kept the man in the corner of his eye and knew that he was still staring, probably now looking puzzled and uncertain. This happened to Dougal often, but he had hoped this place was sufficiently isolated for his presence to be so unlikely it would not be noticed. Anyway, the man left before he did, without approaching him. But that was no guarantee he had not put a name to the face and was talking about it even now.

He must read on. There might be even less time than he feared.

'*Gratitude worse than witchcraft — conjures up the pale meagre ghosts of dead, forgotten kindnesses, to haunt and trouble him.*'

What rubbish. . . . What he had done last week he had done out of gratitude — to his father perhaps, and his father's friends. He had done what they would have done, and had hoped to please their Shades. The past was composed of facts (and Shades), and gratitude was loyalty to the good ones. He read on, having briefly argued with his author. Now Coleridge was noting his observations of his infant children — one of the first men of genius to do this?

'*The wisdom and graciousness of God in the infancy of the human species — its beauty, long continuance, &c &c. (Children in the wind — hair floating, tossing, a miniature of the agitated Trees, below which they played — the elder whirling for joy, the one in petticoats, a fat Baby, eddying half willingly, half by the force of the Gust — driven backward, struggling forward — both drunk with pleasure, both shouting their hymn of joy.*)'

'Hymn of Joy' — people didn't say things like that any more. So much the worse for them. Dougal remembered his pleasure in the early years of his own son, with pain, but he was used to the pain that seemed always to accompany his rememberings. To distract himself he underlined the word 'eddying', because he had relished it, and then stood up. Placing the lamp again on the floor he went to the window and looked out cautiously. It was almost, he thought, as though he were impatient for them to come.

Even if they knew where he was it would take them a couple of days to get here. He had that much start. He should not have lit the fire, or the lamp. But if he sat in the dark and shivered, by the time they arrived he would be a craven wreck. Surely he was safe tonight?

Disembarking from the little ferry — he had been the only passenger — he had walked along the green valley to the last inhabited farm on this part of the island. There he had told the farmer that he had come to borrow Norman Cudforth's cottage, in order to work undisturbed. Perhaps, he had asked the farmer, he could discourage any strangers who came asking for him? Tell them no one was there, perhaps? The farmer had said nothing, merely regarded him from under enormous brows that looked inappropriate, as though stuck on. Curious cat the man

9

had. Its fur was all matted as though covered in glue; the man said it had been bitten by a rat. . . . He had told the farmer that he had a key to the cottage, which was not true. He did not know whether the farmer believed him, and doubted whether he would help with the strangers. Probably he did not care for Norman Cudforth, or his friends. That was understandable.

However, he had let him continue up the valley alone, watching him from his doorway — Dougal had turned and waved — until he was out of sight. When he reached the village, now entirely deserted, it was easy to tell which was Norman's cottage. It was the only one with a roof. He had been able to fumble with the flimsy lock unobserved, but was oddly nervous. Partly because of what he was doing — breaking and entering — but more because of the desolation and extraordinary beauty of the place. He was at the side of the abandoned village, at the head of a green glen. On three sides of him were hills and on the fourth side was the green sea, fringed by cliffs, red and gold, sunset-coloured. And among these scattered, roofless cottages he must have been visible for miles, kneeling outside the only restored one doing something with the lock.

He became certain he was being watched, from the sea. He thought quickly how he could explain his lock-picking: he would say that on his way to the cottage he had dropped and mislaid the key. He forced himself to look round and face the sea; it was green and fierce and empty. No boat could venture out on that. Yet he had seen a movement.

At last the padlock gave; he was fairly sure he had not picked it, it had simply broken, rotted by salty air. Before going into the cottage he decided to walk, as carelessly as he could, to the shore, because the sensation of being watched continued, it seemed to lie on his skin and make it prickle.

He picked his way over tiny, wrecked fields, through bogs that had once been streams, between stone houses, single-storied, roofless, or with a span of roof remaining at a gable-end, the rest bare rafters. he stepped on to the sand and turned to look back up the glen. The colours dazzled him:

the smooth green hills that ended, on either hand, in rose and gold cliffs, the bright yellow strand he stood on, and behind him the sea, a different green, with threatening white flecks. It was the most beautiful place. . . . No wonder men had settled here for a thousand years. He felt a sudden exaltation. He did not care if he was being watched, or by whom.

To shelter from the wind he climbed the bank and went inside a cottage that was still partly roofed. The wooden door of a mildewed wall-cupboard flapped and creaked, there were ashes in the hearth and a scythe stuck in the thatch as though whoever had put it there had expected to use it next day. The place had echoes of life still in it, a feel of having been struck by a sudden visitation.

But Norman in Dublin, enthusiastic about his new cottage, had told his half-bored audience that this was not so. The last families had lingered on until about twenty years ago, but most of the young had drifted to the mainland. Two of the last remaining children were drowned, and the few survivors lost heart and left. Dougal hoped they now had television sets and some comfort, secretly regretting the Saga simplicity of the lives they must have led. Could he have stuck it himself? He remembered what had brought him here.

In Dublin he had been looking at Coleridge's *Notebooks* in a strange state of mind. He had no idea where he was going to go. He knew it would be safest to be out of Ireland for a while so he had climbed onto a plane, leaving a brief note for Lara, who was ill, beyond his reach, and anyway what could he have told her? That he had read a sentence in an old author that had strangely thrilled him? —

'*A subject for a romance — in finding out a desert city & dwelling there.*'

He had remembered Norman's tale of his lonely cottage: how he went there to paint in the summer. He did not like Norman, or his paintings, but it was not summer; Norman would presumably not be there and his cottage sounded a good place to hide.

Well, *could* he dwell here? Dougal, laughing at himself a little, realised that he had seldom been happier.

There was still glass in the little window by the hearth that looked out onto the sea, blurred with salt. He walked over to it.

Surely he had seen a movement? There . . . in the sea. He rubbed the window with his sleeve. A head! It re-appeared, a black-capped bather, inshore. It was a seal. He had been right to feel watched, it was looking up at the window.

He stepped out of the cottage and now there were two seals, now three. He walked along the shore and they accompanied him, wise-looking, benevolent. He was glad of their company. Were they not thought to contain the souls of dead sailors? He climbed back to Norman's cottage and turned at the door, to say goodbye. The green waves were smashing against the boulders on the beach, leaving them slick and black like the heads of the seals. But the seals were comfortable in all that turmoil and still watched him. He waved to them gratefully before he went in.

The cottage smelled of damp and paraffin. It was sparsely furnished but seemed to have everything necessary, some fuel, some tins of food.

The next day Dougal spent almost entirely inside it, as rain bounced like hail off the corrugated iron of the roof. He wondered when the wind would drop. If he had known that it seldom did on the island he would have been more dismayed than he was. Occasionally he felt small spasms of fear. They would never forgive him for what he had done, they would reach him somehow. But the certainty, and the tireless wind, made him oddly sleepy. He dozed often, in his chair, and dreamed dreams of great security and comfort.

It was only on the evening of his second day on the island that he felt equal to opening Coleridge. Then, after reading intently for a while he laid the book on his lap, finger still marking the place, as though it was in braille, and stared at the fire. '*Prayer*', was how the entry began. '*First stage — the pressure of immediate calamities without earthly aidance makes us cry out to the invisible.*' Yes, it does, he thought, listening to the wind. He looked down and read again what followed:

'*Second Stage — the dreariness of visible things to a mind beginning to be contemplative — horrible Solitude.*' No. He remembered with satisfaction the lift of the heart he had felt when he'd been confronted by the beauty of the bay. As for the 'solitude' he was so far rather enjoying it. ·

'*Third Stage — Repentance & Regret — & self-inquietude.*' He was at that stage all right. Maybe he'd skipped the second. . . .

'*Fourth Stage — The celestial delectation that follows credent prayer*' Or any concentrated self-recollection? He smiled when he found himself making verbal distinctions in Coleridge's manner. Then the smile vanished and his face went blank as he read on: '*Fifth Stage — Self-annihilation — the Soul enters the Holy of Holies.*'

'No,' he said aloud, putting aside the book. He always stuck at that point. He had clung to his 'personality' since childhood. It earned him his living. How could he relinquish that? Yet everyone always said you had to. It was a puzzle. . . . Anyway, what did Coleridge — that *mess!* — know about that chilling de-personalisation '*The Holy of Holies*'? he read on for a little but was too disappointed to concentrate. He decided to go to bed.

This was a box-like compartment set in the wall that divided the cottage in two. Norman had lined it inside like a casket, with coloured rugs of a South American appearance.

Dougal checked that the front door was bolted. It was, but not to much purpose. Norman had put four panes of glass in the upper part of the door; you only had to break one of these and you could slide the bolt from the inside. He could not padlock the bolt because he had broken the padlock.

Going back into the room where he had been sitting he kicked off his shoes and climbed, clothed, into the box-bed; if disturbance came he preferred to be dressed. It was damp, mould-smelling, he had had to spread his raincoat over the ethnic blankets, but he delighted in it, it was like a burrow. It even had curtains, which he drew, and lay in perfect darkness, his hands behind his head. The tin roof gave a rattle that was constant, as though the wind, unimpeded by anything on the island, did not gust, simply ignored the tiny obstacle the cottage was.

Lying here within a box inside a box was like a picture of his life, he thought. He'd always liked to assert his 'self' — to hell with Coleridge on that score, anyway for the moment — and then take cover. As a boy he'd liked to lie behind hummocks of grass or unseen in depressions of the ground; had dabbled in small streams and springs, his face close to them, as though he wanted to climb inside. This was mostly in order to forget his mother, who made him miserable. And the wind outside was like the Furies, trying in vain to reach him. Didn't the Furies pursue Orestes because he had killed his mother?. . .

He opened his eyes. Something nagged, at the back of his mind. He was remembering the wall he had stared at when he looked up from his reading; there had been a pile of objects against it: books, papers, boxes. One of the boxes had a certain shape. . . .

Opening the curtains he swung his feet out of the box and groped for matches. Striking one he went to the wall and there it was, strapped, not locked. He undid the buckles and saw inside, nestled in blue velvet, a surprisingly new-looking .22 rifle. He struck more matches and found, grunting with satisfaction, a box of ammunition. The gun had a magazine. He loaded it full, put on the safety-catch and climbed back into bed with it, laying it carefully along his side. He drew the curtains again, laid his right arm along the barrel of the gun and, with one last memory of a Coleridge remark that made him laugh out loud, as well as groan — *'I would glide down the rivulet of quiet life, a Trout'* — he slept.

In the morning he was woken by the noise of glass, breaking.

2

The sudden waking in complete darkness inside his curtains, and the almost simultaneous memory of where he was and why, made Dougal more decisive than he would have been at any other time or place. That, and the feel of the small rifle lying along his side, which grasped. If there was a rivulet of quiet life he had not found it yet and was not going to give up the search without a fight.

He heard the bolt slipped, whispers that sounded less than fierce and the front door being pushed cautiously inwards. Wind filled the room, he heard papers flying about, everything rattled. He manoeuvred the rifle inside his dark space — knocking his eye-socket painfully with the butt — and poked the barrel through the curtains, parting them slightly.

He found he was looking into a small foxed mirror on the opposite wall. He could just make out a man with his back pressed against the bottom end of the box-bed, which formed a passage to the door, looking sideways into the room. Behind him there was another face, apparently that of a woman.

'Good God!' he said, pushing the curtains apart with the gun, laying it on the bed and stepping down into the room. 'Come in!'

'Good God!' said Norman Cudforth, peering cautiously round the bunk-head and seeing Dougal.

'Exactly. I say, would you mind shutting the door? I promise I won't shoot you.' There was an element of farce already: the wind, tugging, was like a roomful of kittens. The moment the door was shut, with a tinkle of the

15

remaining glass, there was a comparative calm that seemed for a moment like perfect silence.

'Sorry you had to break the glass,' said Dougal as Norman, followed by the girl, stepped cautiously into the room. 'Sorry about the gun.' He pulled on his shoes, standing first on one leg, then on the other, smiling, thinking fast.

'How did you know of this place?' Norman stood in the middle of the room, panting a little; also, Dougal noted, embarrassed.

'Everyone does, Norman. You're famous . . . I thought you only used it in the summer. To work. Alone.' Norman glanced quickly at the girl. Good, thought Dougal, I need all the leverage I can get. She did not seem very attractive, fair hair in a frizz of corkscrew wisps, rough-looking hooded coat and bare feet in thonged sandals. . . . These last meant they must have driven up in a car! But he had heard no car. What a rotten fugitive he was! But this damned wind drowned everything.

He yawned deliberately, ruffled his hair, grinned. 'Look, shall I make some coffee?

'God, I'd love some,' said the girl, flatly. 'I'll do it, while you two get on with your explanations.'

Dougal waited till she moved confidently to the gas-ring — not very visible among the books and stacked canvases — before he said, looking at Norman, 'Shall I show you where everything is?'

'Mary Cazenove,' said the other man, heavily. 'Doing some drawings of the island.'

Dougal smiled politely towards the girl who had her back to him. She did not turn. Good, he thought again. Things seemed slightly tipped his way. He had Norman on the defensive. He felt suddenly cheerful, less weary than for years. It was a long time since he had had to think so quickly on his feet. 'D'you mind if I sit down?

'Be my guest . . .'

What an ass Norman was. Dougal tried to remember if he had ever teased Norman in the past. Most people did, it was irresistible. He hoped he hadn't. He might need his help. However, keep him on the wrong foot, for now. The only decent chair was the one he had sat in last night, so he took it, leaving Norman a broken-backed kitchen one.

He bent forward and blew the ashes into a small, reluctant glow. 'Damned cold your hideaway.'

'Look! What the devil are you doing here?'

'Hiding.'

'Who from?'

'The Irish Republican Brotherhood — or whatever they call themselves these days.'

'Good God! But I thought you rather sympathised with them?

'In a way.'

'Then —'

'I heard they were going to put a bomb in Wolfgang Schmidt's car.'

'He's a bastard,' said Mary, stirring coffee at the stove, looking, not very earnestly, for more cups. Dougal wished she would hurry. 'Amalgamated Holdings.'

'Oh, *him*!' said Norman.

'It was to be timed to go off when he was in the car with his family.'

'Ghastly,' said Mary. 'That's war. Sugar?'

'No thanks' said Dougal. She held the mug a little way from him, so that he had to stretch for it. An independent lass, Mary Cazenove. . . . He rather approved of the way she made it clear she was making coffee for herself, pouring other cups absently, reluctantly.

'How did you get this information?' Norman continued his interrogation, suspicious.

'They told me.'

'You? Why?'

'Bloody fools!' said Mary, squatting in front of the now burning fire, blowing on her coffee. Dougal resisted an impulse to offer her his chair.

'I'm not sure. I was at school with some of them. During Grizelda's democratic phase. Before my father took me away.'

17

'Your mother,' breathed Norman reverently. 'Marvellous woman! One of the great figures of old Ireland!'

It was like Norman to be taken in by that warped termagant Grizelda, thought Dougal.

'I passed on the information,' he said. 'They are now in prison awaiting trial. The police found quite a bit of stuff in their houses I believe. Quite a few people, too.'

'I heard of the arrests,' said Mary quietly. 'So you sneaked on your friends?'

'My friends? Yes, I suppose so.'

Mary turned to Norman. 'Schmidt. He's the one who puts up those ghastly holiday bungalows along the coast. Has one of his own — a funk-hole from the Bomb — acres, surrounded by barbed wire, in Kerry. They picketed one of his factories. Non-union. Underpaid. He's a swine.'

Norman said nothing, staring at Dougal.

Dougal felt tired again. He had felt tired ever since that boy had approached him in the bar — he had thought he was come to ask him for his autograph — and had begun to boast of his Republican connections; then he had let slip the plan of assassination.

Dougal had known at once he was trapped. Trapped between two parts of his life, two parts of his own nature, even. He would have to pass on the information — it was too horrible not to. But he had known even then — he had felt sick, looking down into the pale, rather vacant face of the boy — that he would not do it primarily to save Schmidt. He would do it because it was the course of action most destructive to himself. He would do it because his own life had somehow run aground.

So he had gone to Peter, friend of the hearty bare-kneed school his father had sent him to in England, which, despite his great love of his father, he had been even less attached to than his first, Irish one. So now he was aligned with Peter and his kind. Publicly.

He would also now be under surveillance from Peter's men — he consorted with bombers did he not? — while the others, the Seamuses and Terences and Declans would, quite simply, kill him.

18

Something of the last part of these thoughts seemed to be occurring to Norman whose mouth was beginning to sag open.

'Christ!' he said. 'That gun. You slept with it! You must think they know you're here!'

'They might work it out.'

'How?'

'Well, you know Grizelda. She knows about this cottage. She would think it her duty to tell them.'

'Your *mother*?' Norman was appalled.

'Grizelda. Yes.'

'What a little family of grasses you are, to be sure,' said Mary, to the wall above the stove.

'But for God's sake!' said Norman. 'If they find you here they'll kill us too!'

'Sorry about that.' Dougal stared at Mary's back. She was breaking eggs into a pan. A sizzling noise began.

She said, without turning: 'I think we'd better have some breakfast first, don't you?'

Admirable woman, thought Dougal. Like his mother. Norman was breathing noisily. 'How long d'you think we've got?' he asked.

'They might be crossing on the ferry now,' said Dougal. 'Or they may follow false trails for a week — a month. I tried to lay a few.'

'You must see it's damned awkward for us!'

Dougal now smelt bacon. 'I do,' he said, 'and I'm sorry. When I thought of this place it didn't seem likely to involve anybody else.'

'We've got to get out of here!'

Mary said, her back still turned to them: 'Mind if we have breakfast first? Two ferry-crossings in a morning, and nothing to eat. I couldn't do it.' She now began putting food on plates. Three plates, Dougal noted, with relief.

'I don't think you know what these men are like, Mary. They're killers.' Norman stood at the edge of the window, forking food into his mouth, cautiously looking out.

19

Mary seated herself calmly in his chair, still in her hairy overcoat, bending over her plate short-sightedly. 'I thought you were on their side?'

'Uh?' Norman turned back to the room, plate in one hand, fork in the other. He raised them both slightly, then let them fall back in a baffled gesture. 'When it comes to being gunned down, because of a fluke . . . I want out. And that's where we're going.'

'I think you're wise,' said Dougal, finishing his food, rising and collecting the other two plates. He filled a kettle from the cannister of water and put it on the stove to heat.

Behind Dougal's back Mary stared coolly at Norman and he returned her look. He was aware he was not cutting a good figure. Well, he thought, so be it. . . .

When Dougal half-swivelled round, glancing from one to the other, Norman's irritation broke.

'It's no good pointing your bloody actor's profile at us! This isn't one of those god-awful plays you ponce your way through, raising an eyebrow here, shooting a cuff there!'

'They haven't written plays like that for years,' said Mary, judicially.

'He makes every play he's in . . .' began Norman, but he broke off. 'And what the hell are you taking his side for? Coming here in open sandals and complaining about the cold!'

'I didn't feel inspired to kit myself out for a northern idyll.'

Dougal went back to his washing-up. He could not be certain of Norman's support, therefore he must do his best to win over Mary. A small contingency plan was forming in his mind.

Norman had always disliked Dougal's capacity for amused, possibly mocking, silences, and for the way women looked at him. Mary was looking at him now.

In fact she was noticing the way Dougal washed, in the small plastic basin, only two sets of the things they had used. One set he left dirty. He picked up the bowl and, after a second's hesitation, went to the door and threw the

20

water away on the wind. When he returned he put the clean crockery back on the shelf, leaving one dirty set by the stove. He saw Mary's interest and smiled at her. 'Don't you think I would have made a good murderer?'

'Why shouldn't you have used all those things yourself — instead of washing up?' Mary seemed impervious to the smile, which vanished for a moment. Dougal appeared genuinely puzzled, as though something had not happened which should have done, and he could not remember what. Then the smile came back. Mary noticed that his eyes, though they looked straight at you, were unfocused, concentrating on some point behind your head. As though, she thought, you were a partner in a stage-scene and he was trying to remember his lines.

'I hadn't thought of that,' he said.

Norman, watching them, admitted to himself that the man had charm, and did not waste it. Dougal had never looked at him like that. Clearly Dougal wanted Mary for an ally.

'There are lots of things I don't think of,' he was saying to her. 'I daresay,' she said.

'Well — shall we be off?' Dougal became brisk.

'You aren't coming with us, are you?' Norman cursed himself for the squeak in his voice.

'That was considerate about the plates,' said Mary, ignoring him.

'But unnecessary, as you say. Norman, you haven't a little haversack, have you?'

Quickly, trying to make amends, Norman went to the wall and unhooked a fisherman's bag, with a strap.

'Perfect!' Dougal picked up his Coleridge and put it inside, together with one or two other things — toothbrush, pyjamas — which he took from a small overnight bag he had brought with him. Examining the shelf he took down a packet of oatmeal biscuits. 'May I?'

'Of course. Planning a reading tour?'

'You never know. I've never been in this situation before. Difficult to know what to pack.' His eye fell on a half-finished bottle of whisky. 'I wonder if . . . ?'

'Why not?' said Norman drily. Dougal put in in his bag

and retrieved from the interior of the bunk his dark green raincoat of oiled cotton, the kind well-to-do pheasant-shooters wear. This he put on, and a green tweed hat which he pulled well down over his forehead. Then he slung the bag over his shoulder, looked amiably at Norman standing by the window, at Mary still sitting on her hard kitchen chair, and said: 'Well? The sooner the better, don't you think?'

Mary, still in her coat, stood up. Norman, also coated, stayed where he was. 'So you *do* want us to leave together!'

'Not exactly. I mean, I won't stay with you. I thought I might climb up the side of the glen and walk along the tops above the road. That way I can see if anything's going on. You drive to the ferry and if you find anyone walking along the road — I imagine yours is just about the only car hereabouts?' — Norman nodded — 'clever of you to get it — if you meet anyone hold them up a little. They'll probably flag you down, if it's the Boyos. I'm sorry about that, but they won't do you any harm. Get them — if you would — as involved as you can in conversation, while I make myself scarce. Tell them your cottage has been broken into, you're going to the mainland to get a new lock, new glass, that sort of thing. . . . There isn't a policeman on the island, is there?'

'Would you like us to call them when we get across?' asked Mary.

Dougal shook his head. 'No. Have the place buzzing with coppers. They'd certainly shoot me then. They're brave buggers. . . .' His voice trailed away.

Norman, relenting slightly, said, 'Look. Why *don't* you come with us?'

Dougal again shook his head. 'The odd thing is — I feel I've a better chance here. I might be able to meet them. Face to face I mean. Might be able to talk to them.' For the first time he realised he had no idea of what he intended to do, that he was making all this up as he went along. What he *wanted* to do was get out of the bloody wind and read Coleridge. . . .

Mary, detecting his sudden uncertainly, made her voice hard. He had brought this on himself. 'Is there *anything* we

22

could do for you over there?' She had already decided, once
it was certain that men were indeed after him — the whole
thing might be an elaborate joke on Norman; he was the kind
of man who invited such things — that she would telephone
Dougal's wife, Lara, and tell her where he was, if she didn't
know. You can't leave a man to be hunted, and do nothing.

'There's nothing you *could* do, I'm afraid,' Dougal was
saying.

She felt the need to shake him, to rattle his composed
defencelessness — standing there looking like Robert
Donat in the old film of *The Thirty-Nine Steps*.

'You had a choice, didn't you? Between your poor Irish
friends and your rich English ones. You chose the rich
ones. Maybe you always have.'

Dougal was silent.

Mistaking his abstraction for dismay Mary felt a slight
movement of warmth towards him. The island was thousands
of acres of hill and bog. He was throwing himself on its mercy.
Norman, thinking much the same, said: 'But this is awful!'

It was the kind of scene that Dougal had played
professionally many times. He smiled cheerfully: 'Not at
all. Now remember. Keep them talking — if they turn up.
Speak quietly so that they have to poke their heads inside
the car. If you see me on the hills, behind their backs, don't
move your eyes towards me and give me away. Just give me
time to get out of their sight. I'll be watching, because you
may meet nobody and I don't want to run till I have to.'

'Would you like my gun?'

'No thanks. I'll trust to my wits, such as they are. Now —
shall we?'

He led the way and they followed. Outside, the wind
nearly doubled them up, their eyes watered.

'I'm going up there,' Dougal shouted, holding on to his
hat and jerking his head to the hills on the east side of the
glen. 'Give me time to climb a bit. Look in your boot, in
your engine, anything for ten minutes We may be watched,
I don't know. Shake your fists at me — "Never darken my
door again" — that sort of thing. Don't want to look too
pally.' He set off towards the strand and they watched him,

23

not shaking their fists; and then, rather shame-faced, they looked at each other.

'It seems craven — just to turn round and go home,' shouted Mary, the wind pulling at the flesh on her face.

'You'd prefer to stay?' Norman called back, furious with her for putting the whole responsibility on to him.

She looked past him to the hillside, where Dougal, already a small figure, darker than the green of the high hill, was beginning his climb. 'It may be a trick of his, just of get us out of the house.'

'You heard of the arrests.'

She shrugged. 'He'd have heard of them too.'

'If it's true,' he bellowed, his voice coming fitfully to her, though they stood only a few feet apart, 'and they arrive, they'd know he'd been here. Footprints, or something. They'd know. So we'd be conspirators, against them.'

'We are already.'

'So you want to stay?'

She shook her head, doubtfully.

'Well then, let's go.'

'As you wish,' she said.

'No!' he snarled. 'As *we* bloody wish!'

Like all actors Dougal was fit. It is not a sedentary trade. But he was hot and puffing by the time he reached the tops of the hills. The wind astonished him. It grew in violence with every step he took upward; it seemed to have arms, it grappled with him, an invisible octopus. He braced his legs against it, butted his head into it, he had no time to think or see, entirely preoccupied with the struggle. Indeed, it seemed to blow every thought out of his head, as though it blew in one ear and out the other, taking with it his brain-cells. He wondered if it was possible to be driven mad by unrelenting wind. The day was reasonably fine. In shelter it would have been impossible to imagine the violence of the moving air.

He looked down and saw Mary and Norman climb into their car. He had ruined their trip and forced them to help him. Well — it was the last help he was likely to get.

24

He could only account for the exhilaration and freedom that he felt, battling along the top of the hill, wind-flattened heather tearing at his ankles, by imagining that the wind, and its noise, had made him light-headed — how on earth was he going to survive in it? On the other hand, how dull and miserable his life must have become if this, so far, was so much better!

The car started along the road below, slowly, keeping pace with him. Good. He could now see the sea on the other side of the island, where the water was even more broken, dangerous. Perhaps there would be no ferry in this wind? But he remembered the one he had crossed in, a small motorboat; he had stood, legs apart, hanging on to a bulkhead in the tiny deckhouse, while the ferryman peered through windows white with hissing spray and the radio crackled with what sounded to Dougal like distress signals. Sometimes the boat had taken off altogether, the note of its engine rising as the screw spun in air, then it descended into a hole, with a horrid cracking sound as it hit the water again and the deckhouse grew dark as they were briefly engulfed. Dougal had remembered that the chemist near the quay, when he was buying his toothbrush, had asked him if he was crossing that day and when he said yes had laughed, disconcertingly.

But they had arrived, with another tremendous crash, this time a collision with the jetty.

Now he saw, as he watched the sea, that there was a boat on it, hidden till now in some deep trough of the waves. It was small; no larger, he guessed, than the boat he had crossed in. He blinked his watering eyes and concentrated on that tiny shape. He became sure it was becoming *smaller* — was going back. That meant someone had just been landed on the island. The ferries only crossed when there were passengers. Mary and Norman had missed it. They might have a long wait. Perhaps, when they realised this, they could telephone from the solitary farm they were now passing. He lost sight of them for a while as the road went behind the farm, and concentrated again on his struggle with the wind. Having already blown the landscape bare of anything above ankle-height it did not have to gust round corners, nothing shaped or pushed it. Nevertheless, it had a shape of its own. He felt that if it had been coloured he would see it scalloped, or spiked with gusts.

The car emerged from behind the farm. He continued walking — stumbling, staggering, his hat pulled down to his ears.

Two men in raincoats came round the headland and appeared on the road. They walked towards the car.

He would know it was them if they flagged it down.

They did.

Crouching, but exposed, he began to think fast. If Mary and Norman played their parts, and the two men continued along the road to look for him on the other side of the island, he could descend and wait for the ferry with them. His disinclination to do so was only partly a wish not to involve others. From the beginning, he had felt a strong desire to see the whole thing through by himself. He had been very little by himself of late.

Meanwhile he looked to his right. The breadth of the island, as far as he could overlook, offered no cover; not a bush, not a tree. But to his left, below him, between him and the now halted car, was an enormous and solitary boulder. It was hollow. Almost with surprise he realised he had intended to hide there all along. It was a megalithic tomb, though it looked solid from the road, and he had examined it on his first walk from the ferry to the cottage. He would hide there.

The men would soon reach the car. He lay as flat as he could in the heather, high above them. They stopped beside the car, one on either side. Mary and Norman must both have wound their windows down. The men leaned towards them, their heads nearly inside the car. . . .

Dougal ran for it, down the hill towards the boulder.

He reached it, and squeezed inside, without either of the men turning. So far as he could judge Mary and Norman had done their job. He felt slightly surprised at that, as he carefully stretched himself inside, panting. After the wind it was very still inside the stone, and by contrast it was warm, as though centrally heated. His cheeks and hands began to burn.

There were two little chambers, smoothly hollowed out; with room, he discovered, for a body in each if you kept your knees bent. Men were smaller in those days. His chamber even had a little ledge at the back of it, a stone pillow. He put his haversack there and rested his head on it. Someone, in eighteenth-century writing, had carved initials very near his eyes.

He listened, and heard the car start.

There was a little path to the tomb, marked with white pegs across the bog, which is why he had first noticed it. Would they see the pegs, and investigate?

He heard, borne on the wind, words exchanged. Then he heard steps splashing along the path. At first he was not sure, then he knew that someone was coming.

In the semi-darkness, bent knees touching the stone roof, he tried to compose himself. A tomb, he reflected, was as good a place to be found in as any. He had put himself inside the final burrow. The starkness of his position gave him something like satisfaction. On a nearly uninhabited island, *inside* the only big stone for miles, in a boggy glen where, he had noticed, there was not even a bird, he waited. But he heard his heart beating. He was afraid.

Then he heard the screech of brakes. Distantly he heard a voice — Norman's — shouting: 'He may be up there!' And then he heard the car drive on.

So Norman had betrayed him, as he left the stage, on an exit line. . . .

The splashing feet had been nearly at the stone. He heard them stop. Heard, to his astonishment, the man shout: 'Hey! You there!' and a similar shout from the man on the road. 'Get after him,' said the man near the stone and the feet splashed away, running.

Then there was silence, or only the sound of the wind outside the stone. Dougal decided it would not be wise to look out. The haversack was uncomfortable under his head so, twisting, he pulled it down, extracting his Coleridge and his biscuits, replaced it and once again settled himself.

27

There was just enough light from the opening by which to read, if he angled the page. He noticed, where the opening met the moist air, a rusty lichen seemed to glow.

He read, skipping, for that was one of the joys of the book, it was like a companion rattling on, you listened or not, as you felt inclined, until your attention was caught:

'*Wednesday — Afternoon. Abed — nervous —*' Yes indeed, he could still feel his own heart beating '*— had noticed the prismatic colours transmitted from the Tumbler — Wordsworth came — I talked with him — he left me alone — I shut my eyes — beauteous spectra of two colours, orange and violet.*' He would have enjoyed that lichen. He shut his own eyes and inspected the inside of his lids, or was it his retina? He saw a photograph, which faded, of the light in the oblong opening of the tomb '*— which immediately turned to peagreen & then gradually grew to my eye into a beautiful moss, the same as is on the mantelpiece at Grasmere.*'

Grasmere was where Wordsworth lived. So Coleridge 'abed — nervous' is remembering happy times in his friends' cottage. Dougal tried to cast his own mind back to happy times but could not for the moment think of any; he was, he realised, too scared. He clung to Coleridge like a raft.

He read on, skipping pages of Latin, rhyme-schemes, notations of metres and then jerked up so violently he cracked his head on the roof:

'*A Hollow place in the Rock like a Coffin —*' — Good God! '*— a Sycamore bush at the head, enough to give a shadow for my face, and just at the Foot one tall Foxglove — exactly my own length — there I lay and slept — It was quite soft. June 18.1801 Thursday.*'

No sycamore, no foxglove. All the same. . . . His skin crept, pleasurably.

There had been no sound from the men for some time. He dared, very cautiously, to peer out. Nothing. A thin rain, blown into mist, was swirling about. He put his head right out of the rock and could just see two figures climbing up the other side of the glen.

Why they were doing this he could not imagine. Anyway, they wouldn't find him up there. Then, presumably, they would try the cottage. He must not move till they came down again, rejoined the road, and pushed on to Norman's place, with their backs to him. Before that any movement at all would stand out in this bare place. He would give them an hour. Then, not having found him at the cottage, they might come back and be inspired to look inside the stone. He would no longer be there. Meanwhile he was warm (fairly) and dry, and could do nothing. So he returned to Coleridge, and laughed:

'*Something inherently mean in action.*' What a companion he was! '*Even the Creation of the Universe disturbs my Idea of the Almighty's greatness — would do so, but that I conceive that Thought with him Creates.*'

It was in order to make nothing happen that he had done what he did in Ireland. . . . Meanwhile the Men of Action were toiling up the opposite hillside as he lay snugly here.

'*The unspeakable Comfort to a Good man's mind — nay, even to a criminal to be understood — to have someone that understands one — & who does not feel, that on earth no one does. The Hope of this — always more or less disappointed, gives the passion to Friendship.*'

'Always more or less disappointed' — except by Coleridge. Their minds seemed to be marching together. He had even crawled inside a rock. . . . With part of his mind, while reading, Dougal was considering his position. Yes, better to do nothing for an hour. Then he gasped. Coleridge had said it for him, again: '*better to do nothing than nothings.*'

Meanwhile the two toiling figures had nearly reached the top of the other side of the glen. They had seen a man silhouetted up there. When Norman had called to them to look the shape had ducked down.

Thus at last, out of breath, right hands stuck in their raincoat pockets, they came upon Abraham Muir, regarding them equably, seated under an overhanging rock that more or less sheltered him from the wind and rain, eating a bannock.

3

Her visitors had gone.

Grizelda, slightly adjusting the ornaments on her over-mantel, unaware she was doing so, was profoundly angry. A little white Queen Anne cream-jug she moved, a fraction of an inch, and then the other objects, equally delicate, but of less certain use. Dougal had often watched his mother do this, her back to him, and wondered vaguely what the things had originally been for. It was her habit to fiddle in this way whenever she was trying to conceal irritation, as she usually was in his presence.

This was the first time in her life she had been forced to be anything other than straightforward in her political allegiance. And she had been trapped into it by Dougal, who was too selfish for politics — for any cause other than himself — who had annoyed and distressed her since the day he was born. Indeed, for several months before that.

She put her ringed fingers on the white-painted overmantel and stared down at the ornate, ancient electric fire, frowning.

Was there not a mother of Ancient Rome who had betrayed her son, for the Republic, and been considered an exemplar of Roman virtue?

If she had loved him she might have been able to do it. As it was she would never have been certain that she had not done so out of spite.

She had been pleased when the Commandant had telephoned. She had remembered his father. Did they call themselves 'Commandant' nowadays? She was out of touch — a little.

At first, when he arrived, burly, comfortable-looking, with a rather unimpressive youth who had sat at a distance, on the edge of a hard chair, refusing the offer of a more comfortable one, looking round the room as though he had never seen one like it, she had thought the older man had come to invite her to some planned celebration. It was, as it happened, her father's centenary soon.

He had leaned back in his armchair and said, without surprise, smiling: 'We were followed on our way here.'

'People who come here have been followed for the last sixty years,' she said proudly, returning his smile.

'We know about this house, Mrs Kerr, and the things that have happened in it; what you and your father and *his* father have done and suffered for Ireland.'

Grizelda bowed her head slightly.

'And you, Jamesy?' said the man, turning to the boy, whose mouth fell open. 'Do *you* know? That *The Republican* was printed here, by Mrs Kerr's father, and smuggled to our men in the British dungeons?'

'I do,' said the boy, and licked his lips.

'You see?' said the man, turning back to her. 'They say the Irish have long memories. A conquered people usually has. But we have fine memories, as well as foul. Your family. A noble tradition. Stretching back hundreds of years.' He looked at her intently. He is no fool, she thought. What does he want? 'Generation after generation.'

Grizelda waited, in shadow, her back to the bright window. She lightly touched the leaves of a poinsettia that stood on a low table by her chair.

'Do you see much of Dougal?' said the man, trying to sound as though he was still going through the formalities.

'I'm afraid I never watch television. Or go to the theatre.'

'He comes to see you.' It was a statement.

'Rarely.'

The man looked round at the boy, vaguely. He had not wished to be embarrassed by such news of filial neglect. He sought to bring the interview to its point, which was difficult.

'I was at school with him,' he said. 'Briefly.'

'Were you? His father was a Scotsman, you know. Did not approve of the Christian Brothers. He thought them too strict. So I'm afraid he insisted on sending him to a Scotch,

Protestant, school where, as far as I could judge, they spent most of their time underclad on the tops of mountains. That was meant to be better for them than the strap, apparently. Fitted them to rule an Empire. He was equally out of place there, I'm sorry to say. But we have tended to lose touch.'

'He didn't get on with the Brothers, that's true. But we've kept up with each other.' The man mentally absolved himself from the white lie. He judged it necessary, in the course of duty. He doubted if Dougal Kerr remembered him.

'Really?' said Grizelda.

'You sound surprised.'

'I am, a little.'

'May I ask you why, Mrs Kerr?'

Grizelda could think of many answers: that Dougal preferred more glamorous company was one of them. 'He mixes with — a more superficial type of person.'

'But is he loyal?'

'To what?'

'To the cause?'

'Oh, I shouldn't have thought so. Would you?'

The man rubbed his face. 'The devil of it is, I would,' he said. Then, more briskly. 'Do you know where he is?'

'Dougal? No. Why?'

'I'm afraid we need to see him.'

' "Afraid"! What *can* you mean?'

'Certain information was passed. . . . It led to the arrest of four men.'

Mrs Kerr reached down beside her chair for her handbag and fumbled in it, taking something out. She rose and went to the window and when she turned she was wearing dark glasses. 'You believe my son is an informer?'

The man said nothing, resisting a need to shade his own eyes from the light. She stood, a silhouette, between him and the window.

She sat down again, arranging her skirt, plucking at it.

'How could *he* have any information of importance!' She made no effort to keep the scorn out of her voice.

'I gave it to him,' said the man.

'Then you are a fool!'

33

'It seems so. Yes.' He was profoundly uncomfortable. His eyes rested on the ceiling, on the floor, anywhere but on the disconcertingly masked face of Mrs Kerr. 'I liked him. Your son. Your father's grandson. Was any of your family not to be trusted, in all these hundreds of years?'

'There was somebody once — in Robert Emmett's time. A cousin. He ended badly.' She spoke vaguely, distracted by the first stirrings of an excitement that contained a temptation. It had occurred to her, like a certainty, that she knew where Dougal was. 'I should never have told his *father* anything,' she said.

'Ah,' said the man; it was a small involuntary noise as though he had been slightly winded. He greatly disliked these family revelations.

'But his father was not one of us,' he said. Mrs Kerr was part of his sense of Ireland, like Maud Gonne MacBryde, like the Countess Markievicz — and further back even than that, for his awareness of Irish history sometimes stood beside him like a presence, composed of all who had fought in her cause. He did not want this clear conception marred by hints of discord between wife and husband, between mother and son. Such matters were private.

'Mr MacDermott, what will you do with him? When you find him?' Her voice was soft, reasonable. She was remembering Norman Cudforth at her last little reception. *Such* a good painter. If only Dougal had been an artist. But he had no talent . . . for anything. 'You would not harm him.'

MacDermott leaned forward and put his elbows on his knees. He spread his fingers, examined them and then looked up, forcing a grin. 'A little fright, mebbe.' He purposely let the nasal Dublin note into his voice, almost risking a wink but deciding against it. 'They're very upset at the Unit.'

'With you?'

'And with your son.'

She nodded. Norman had been talking of his cottage, on an island. Dougal had come in late and had seemed oddly interested. . . . *Damn the boy*! 'I'm afraid I cannot help you. As I've suggested, I see little of my son.'

'That's the way it is, nowadays,' said MacDermott, rising. 'And it was much to ask of you.'

'What do you mean "much"!' She stood up; under her coloured cheeks a real colour was burning. She was raging, but not with her interlocutor. He stood, embarrassed. 'Try his theatrical friends,' she said.

'I will.' He bowed slightly, with an odd formality, and took his leave, jerking his head at the boy to follow. Mrs Kerr heard footsteps going down the stairs into the hall, then someone outside the door, gently knocking. It was the boy.

'It was me who blabbed,' he said, breathless. 'He's taking it all on himself. He's my uncle.'

'Why ever did you do such a thing?'

'I'd seen Dougal on the fillums, you see. But don't you fear. We'll find him.' He seemed cheered at the thought. There was a call from below, at the front door, and the boy was gone. She heard the front door slam.

She stood at the fireplace adjusting the ornaments. The soft swish of the traffic in the street below made the room seem particularly silent.

As a little girl she had seen the Countess Markievicz riding in the funeral procession, after the Scottish soldiers had fired into the crowd on Bachelor's Walk. So fine she looked, so high and proud, under the British guns. . . . After that one of her earliest memories was of the executions after the Easter Rising in 1916, so slow and unfeeling, and so secret. 'Like,' a woman said at the time, 'watching blood seeping out from under a door.' *That* had united Ireland! In the Civil War, as a young woman, she had sided with De Valera; Ireland could not be partitioned, must be a Nation. She had worked, given shelter, risked her life, served a (short) prison term. She had never doubted that an insurrection involved, at the outset, the shooting of defenceless people. How else was it to begin? The English had chosen never to understand this. In eighteenth-century America, in India, in Palestine, in Cyprus, in Aden, they called whoever opposed them murderers.

Now her son was a traitor, and she had flinched from handing him over. But it was worse than that. She had been

35

tempted — and in the wrong way! Tempted to revenge herself on him for her own indifference, for the way she had disliked him from the day he was born. She had been unable to help it. And everyone had been so happy for her! — a young bride, a young mother — her subterfuges had made her want to scream. It was taken for granted that she would feel 'naturally' whereas her natural feelings were for the poor, the oppressed, the bewildered; for a noble cause, for sacrifice. Because she was a woman she was expected to forget her own personal nature! It was all the fault of that tweeded, patronising booby she had married, with his Low Church morality, his golfing good nature and his irresistible good looks. At least she had thought them irresistible. *Goose*! In time they were what she came to detest most about him. Nothing — his hair wet in the rain, disarranged by sleeping — nothing could diminish the inane perfection of his face. It became a symbol of her bondage, she wanted to destroy his ignorant composure, force him to twist his face into a snarl. He merely smiled — though she made him flinch, sure enough — and then he took Dougal away, the boy doting on him, looking more and more like him. And now that boy, simulacrum of his father, had made her betray — however complex and impure her feelings — *herself*!

She moved to the telephone, panting. Heaven knew how things were between Lara and that idiot, her son. But there was an oppression in her chest. She needed to speak to somebody.

Though Grizelda Kerr was never to know this — and her part-betrayal both relieved and annoyed her — her suggestion that MacDermott should talk to Dougal's theatrical friends had been unnecessary. He had not really expected to get anything out of her — it would not have been natural — and his next call was to be on Dougal's colleagues in his known haunts. The centre of Dublin is a small and convivial place.

He told Jamesy to run off home because he wanted to give his instinct, his bloodhound nose, a free run and he had to be alone for that. It was also easier, on his own, to throw off their not very competent or interested tail. By quickly turning corners he did this, and by means of the back door of a pub where he was known — and so was Dougal — he made his way to the bar.

Some performers from the Olympia Theatre sat in a group. He greeted them but did not join them. He stood alone, sipping stout, trying to make his mind blank. Things sometimes happened if he did that. 'Dougal Kerr been in?' he asked the barman at last. 'Haven't seen him, Brian. Not this week or two.'

'Dougal Kerr you want?' said a well-dressed man who had just come in.

That was quick, thought Brian, slowly. He examined the man over his glass-brim. He recognised him as an Irish actor who had had some success in England. A television commercial had made him a household face. Brian knew who he was and was fairly certain the man would know who *he* was. That excited a certain sort of person, gave them, he supposed, a sense of being in the know. Brian offered him a drink, which he accepted.

'Seldom comes in here, you know.' The man said it with a sort of cold deference in his voice, as though to suggest that someone as 'grand' as Dougal could hardly be expected to.

'He's changed then?'

'Usually away filming. Somewhere glamorous.' Now the man took his turn to stare at Brian, innocently, his drink to his lips.

'Is he filming now?'

'I think not.'

Then why did you bring it up, my lad? The man interested Brian. He could sense him waiting for the next question. Well — ask it.

'Where would he go,' he said, staring into his stout, 'if he wanted to hide away from the world?'

'You want to find him? What for? I wouldn't want to — '

'No, no,' said Brian gently. 'Just a chat.'

The man frowned, considering. He would come up with

37

something, Brian knew it. He could not know that he had stumbled across the man who hated Dougal most.

For twenty-five years Michael Merry had had to smile and congratulate Dougal when Dougal was given the parts he wanted for himself. Yet he, Merry, was the better actor. It was the justness of his anger that poisoned it. He was talented, dedicated, whereas Dougal cared nothing for his profession, even despised it, and it was this indifference that guaranteed his luck.

Everything about Dougal maddened Michael. Years before, in provincial repertory in England, Dougal had lent him a shirt. It was a very good shirt — Dougal, for all his confidence, needed the extra assurance of good clothes. Within an hour of putting it on Michael had crumpled and soiled it, amazed at the depth of his feeling. Over the years he had been compelled to hark back again and again to this damned shirt! 'It was so good of you, years ago. When my mother washed it she said it was the finest shirt she'd ever handled.' Dougal, whose mother had doubtless never washed a shirt, had been puzzled at first, but as time passed and the shirt kept being mentioned he had begun to laugh at the queer mania of his friend and then talk of something else, while Michael howled inwardly, imploring Dougal to notice the appalling malice that gripped him, so they could become open enemies and he be cleansed. But Dougal remained the same; friendly, indifferent.

Although, once or twice Dougal had wondered. . . . He had lost a part because of a rumour he was a drunk. Then there was the conviction in certain circles that he was a homosexual, which he was not. In New York, on Fifth Avenue, an acquaintance had stopped him, white-faced: 'Good God! I was told you'd died!' 'Who by?' 'Mick Merry.'. . . But Dougal had gone on his way smiling, thinking that Micky was an odd one.

Merry had never been able to touch him, not properly. 'Has he been up to something?' he said, to the patiently waiting Brian.

'We just want to see him. That's all.'

'*We*. It sounds almost a duty to help you.' Merry giggled. 'Yes.'

'Well, I don't know where he is, I'm afraid. . . . But a thought *has* come into my mind.'

Brian waited again.

'If *I* wanted to get away. . . . I've heard the painter, Norman Cudforth, has a lonely cottage on an island. That sounds the sort of place, don't you think? Not that I know Norman all that well. Dougal does. Of course.'

Brian wondered, for the second time that day, at the dislike Dougal Kerr seemed to arouse; in his mother, in this fellow who clearly detested him.

'What island would that be?'

Merry suddenly looked dismayed. 'I — can't remember. . . .'

'Ah, well. Never mind. It shouldn't be difficult to find out. Thanks anyway. Shall I give your regards to Dougal? When we find him?'

'Oh do!'

Out in the street, after a quick glance up and down it, Brian sighed, thinking of the strangeness of human passions. That fellow would sell Dougal for nothing.

About his own task Brian did not think. He had done many things he did not care to think about before, or remember after. He was a soldier.

Inside the bar, when Brian left, Michael Merry went over to join the group in the corner. Except for one, silent, military-looking man of well-known and affectionately received effeminacy, they were younger than he was and gratifyingly pleased at his approach.

'You were a long time with that chap. You know who he is, don't you?'

Michael raised his eyebrows, and grinned.

'What'd he want?'

'Dougal Kerr, apparently.'

'*Dougal?*' The chorus was disbelieving.

'What's he been up to?' said one.

'Whatever it is, I bet he's given himself the best part,' said another.

'A dear boy,' said the military-looking man. 'Such a waste.'

39

Michael said nothing, smiled. He wondered how he would feel about what he had done when he was alone. Anyway, what *had* he done? Put the heavy mob onto Dougal? Delicious, let's be honest about it. What *was* the name of that island? . . .

Grizelda probably thought I was drunk on the telephone just them. . . . Lara always sounded drunk, in her own ears, on the rare occasions when she was forced to speak to Grizelda. In fact it had been the sleeping-pill — she had got up during the night to take another, and it had not worn off.

Well, she was drunk now.

Dougal had said he'd be away, maybe for a while. She'd given the maid a holiday, because she wanted to slip, slide, free-fall to the bottom, undisturbed. Dougal had no idea how often she did this. Or maybe he had. . . . He was away quite a lot. He didn't interfere, anyway. Thank God.

She moved, luxuriously, to put her hands behind her head on the pillow. The seam of her cashmere jersey was torn under one arm. She smelt her own body; it was comforting. She must remember to wash sometime. She must remember what the hell it was that Grizelda had said.

Dougal in some sort of trouble? Or not. As the case may be. She hadn't been very specific. Anyway, it was probably Grizelda who'd caused the trouble, in which case Dougal wouldn't give a damn.

The sounds of Dublin outside were distant, soothing. The room was at the back of the house and looked out on to the backs of other houses. A late blackbird sang on a low television aerial, its voice mellowed, magnified, by the brick walls it bounced off. It was a time of day Lara liked, the silence of the town settling for the evening; an incomplete silence, but somehow thicker, more tangible than rural silences.

Not that she'd heard many of those, she thought. Ma shoved me hard — Brooklyn dancing school, photo-sessions, auditions. . . . We needed the dough, two women alone. I was a woman at eight years old, for Christ's sake! That Grizelda thinks she's tough — she wouldn't last two rounds with Mother! Lara laughed at the thought, then at the memory of the polite disbelief with which Dougal treated Grizelda. God, he was funny with her! And it was the only way, she was truly incredible. Lara loved the way Dougal could make her laugh, even at serious things, like his dislike of his own mother. Anybody else would be under a shrink.

Twelve years ago she'd led him through his first Hollywood part. Was it as long ago as that?. . . Yes, I was twenty-three, two years into that damned contract. . . . *Literally* led him, by the hand, pulled him where I knew the director'd want him. He hadn't minded. His hand had been dry. . . . Yielding, but unresponsive. She had not been used to that. Her leading men, when they weren't faggots — not that she minded, but Dougal wasn't, despite his Englishness she'd known at once he wasn't — were usually sweaty, eager; she was the goal, a career-prize: make her and they would be made. Or they were bastards. Or both. Not that Dougal was a leading-man; second-lead; he didn't get the girl . . .

'Oh-yes-he-di-id. . . .' She almost sang it, out loud, reaching for the tumbler on her bedside table. He got *me* — the poor sod.' The tumbler was empty. She put it back on the table without looking and it fell to the floor, rolling away.

He had seemed to her so wonderfully *English*. '*Christ!*' She laughed aloud in the darkened room. What did she know then of the Scotch and the Irish and the feuds and the bombs and all the bloody history? Not much more than she knew about the other bombs, pointing, all over the world, always in the sky, under the sea . . .

But it wasn't that, it wasn't bombs that had brought her to this, lying on a bed, drunk and smelly. 'That's too easy, girl.' She swung her legs to the floor, blood rising to her head; she sat, hunched, slowly beginning to notice through her stockings that there were dark streaks between her toes. '*I'm disgusting!*' she said, in her husky voice, without disgust.

She picked up the fallen tumbler, overbalancing, pushing herself up from the carpet with one hand, went uncertainly to the bathroom and stood staring down at the bath-taps.

41

One wall was a mirror and she looked up quickly, to catch herself off-guard, to see how she was getting on with her half-conscious ambition, which was the destruction of her famous beauty, her tyrant. To herself, at least, she did not seem to be doing badly: her fair hair stuck to her scalp in dark strands, there was a puffy look about her mouth and her eyes seemed to have become smaller, as though they had retreated inside her head.

She turned on the hot tap in the cold bathroom and immediately steam obscured her image.

In the kitchen she poured herself another drink. No, it wasn't bombs or the state of the lousy world. Maybe she wanted to give herself a childhood at last?' — Maybe climb right back inside! But to hell. . . . It wasn't Dougal either. He was just fine. As empty as she was, maybe. Anyone with a mother like that had to be loused-up somewhere. But he kept going, was fun to be with, kind. No, not kind — *intelligent*.

He'd not been around much of late, or never for long. Busy. Busy? No. She made him nervous, as though he thought what afflicted her was catching. She laughed, holding her drink, scratching her scalp and then examining her fingernails.

'Damn!'

The telephone was ringing *again*. It never rang. All calls were channelled through Dougal's agent. He told her there were quite a few, that in her 'retirement' she'd become a kind of Garbo. Dougal made her clean up every few weeks and took her out to dinner, so that people wouldn't think he'd done her in and hidden her body in a trunk.

She took the receiver of the ringing telephone off its hook and dropped it on the floor, could hear some woman calling her surname. Then she pushed her way through the bathroom steam and peered down into the bath. She had forgotten to put in the plug.

She went back to the bed and lay on it. What had Grizelda been trying to say? That Dougal in some way might need her? They were not like that, either of them, *needing* each other in that spooky way. He certainly needed her help with his acting. . . . But not in any other way. Not Dougal.

She had a vague memory that he'd told her where he'd gone. Written it down somewhere. What had that awful woman been trying to say . . . ?

'There's no reply,' said Mary to Norman, through the open door of the telephone box in the freezing hall of the hotel. Young men, bulging inside their buttoned suits, their hair plastered down, each with a half-bottle of whisky in his pocket, pushed through the swing door every few moments, bringing with them each time a separate gust of icy air, as though it was their personal climate. They lurched past Norman and Mary, anticipation in their eyes, heading for an asbestos annexe marked 'ballroom'.

'The Fleet's in,' said Norman, flattened against Mary as the men shoved past. She still held the receiver.

'It rang and then stopped,' she said. 'Then there was a sort of thump.'

'She probably fell down.'

'Who?'

'That crazy wife of his. If Grizelda gave us the right number.'

'Lara Gray? Is she crazy?'

'Barking. Drunk too.'

'She has everything! Beauty, fame, money. What do these people *want* . . .'

'Well . . .' said Norman wondering if she seriously expected him to answer. 'I don't suppose you want a dance in the shed, do you? It's tied down with ropes to stop it blowing away. Well. That seems about it then. Doesn't it?'

'About what?'

'We've done what we can. Let's try some dinner.'

'I couldn't eat.'

'Shall we go up, then?' he said, his spirits rising a little. 'I've booked a double-room.'

'Really.'

'Look!' he exploded. 'I've been standing about in this

43

bloody hall all day while you contact Dublin which no one on the island seems to have heard of. Then we do three rounds with a typhoon while you commune with your conscience — about whether to call Lara Gray — at the top of your bloody voice. Now I'm standing here assaulted by an anthology of fish-smells while about four trawler-loads of splendid seafaring men walk over and through me. I've had enough of Dougal Kerr to last me a lifetime. Do you want to eat, or go to bed?'

'Neither.'

'Well *I'm* going to eat and you can either watch or get beaten up outside by flying chimney pots, or by belaying pins I shouldn't wonder. It's a Force Nine gale and the lads are looking for action. Perhaps you'd like to stand outside and watch the Ballroom take off?'

Reluctantly she followed him into a small malodorous dining-room. It was empty, without windows and music came from loudspeakers.

'*Christ*!' he said, momentarily halted by the noise and the smell.

'We can't just leave him to those men,' she said, as they sat down.

He spoke through clenched teeth. 'Mary. We could be in my cottage. We're not. We're here. Just for that, as far as I'm concerned, those men can push him off a cliff.'

Mary got up and made her way to the empty reception desk. At least she could get herself a single-room.

Norman, alone, noisily clattered his knife and fork. A waitress leaned against the wall, picking at her nails, talking to someone invisible. She did not look up.

If he could get some food inside himself he might still be able to save the evening. A thought struck him. He glanced surreptitiously at his watch. Dinner couldn't be over by seven o'clock, could it? Too bloody true it could. . . . He changed his scowl to a diffident, pleading grin as the waitress, still talking over her shoulder, began to move, approximately in his direction.

4

After misinforming the two strangers, and watching them disappear in the wrong direction, Abraham Muir slowly made his way down the hillside, keeping his eyes on the stone. Nothing quite so interesting had happened since the Second World War.

For a while he sat on a boulder, contemplating it. Then, approaching nearer he called out, in a high monotone that seemed designed to pierce the wind: 'You in there. You can come out. Your friends are gone.'

There was a pause, then Dougal slowly put his head out. He saw a small, thick man in an old gaberdine raincoat and a cap, who looked at him impassively. He had the appearance of a retired grocer.

'You're sure?' he said, daftly.

'Ay.'

He carefully climbed out and then stood, rubbing his behind, flexing his legs and arms. The wind, about which he had nearly forgotten inside the stone, caught in his ears and gave him a sort of thunderous gusting deafness. With difficulty he remembered where he was, and why. Immediately he felt exposed. 'Mind if I join you? Wherever you're going?'

The man showed no disposition to move. 'That stone is an old tomb.'

'Yes.' Dougal splashed down towards him, held out his hand. 'My name is Dougal Kerr.'

'Ay.' What did *that* mean? The man took his hand, shook it, but kept his own name to himself. 'You didn't want to be meeting your friends, likely?'

'No. . . . Look, I still don't. D'you mind if we move?'

The rain fell. The man seemed not to notice. 'They'll be

45

a while. They went that way.' He indicated with a slight movement of his head, not taking his eyes off Dougal.

'D'you think?. . .' Dougal made a small movement of his head in the opposite direction. But still the man stood, enjoying himself.

At last he turned and set off down the hill. He was wearing ordinary shoes, but somehow the water seemed not to fill them. His clothes made Dougal feel he was dressed ridiculously, like a hiker in a High Street. 'They're not the polis?' said the man, not turning, his voice borne thinly on the wind.

'No.'

'I thought they were not. We don't have the polis often.' There was the air of a respectable brigand about him. Dougal's spirits, in his company, were slowly rising.

They reached the little jetty and the coast road. 'Will there be another ferry today?' said Dougal, looking at the spray dashing against it.

'Maybe.'

'Are you often cut off?'

'They're cut off from us, sometimes.' The man gave him a glance and the shoulders of his raincoat rose two or three times. He was laughing. 'Will you walk with me?'

'Gladly,' said Dougal, adopting what he hoped was a tone of equal formality.

Their road had bog on one hand, rising to hills, and on the other was the sea, a surprising calm one when it was close in. There was even a little beach from which they startled black and white birds which rose up, protesting. But further out it was rough. A single freighter lurched up, far away, and then disappeared into a trough, as though it had sunk.

'They call it Hell's Kitchen,' said the man, seeing him look.

Dougal, professionally interested, admired the way he projected his voice, without raising it. The monotone was useful, no words died away. It seemed to come from the back of the palate. He tried it himself. 'What's your name?'

'You'll not be from these parts?' the man said, as though by way of reply. Dougal was not to be permitted such intimacy yet. He stopped unexpectedly, so that Dougal slightly bumped into him. 'Betty Corrigal's grave,' he said. A cormorant stood by the road, looking startled, its head-feathers flattened by the wind. It tried to take off but the wind blew it down again. The man was pointing to a bleak little lake at the side of which there was a roughly fenced enclosure and a cross of two sticks. 'Digging peat we found her coffin. I opened it. Officially. I was post-master.'

I bet his Post Office had a shop, thought Dougal, triumphant. I was right, he's a sort of hermit grocer.

'She was dry to the touch, like a mummy. No parish would have her, a hundred years ago, so they put her in a bog.'

'Why?'

'She was with child. First she tried to hang herself, then she drowned herself. She lived there.' He pointed to a pile of stones.

Dougal liked the way the man knew her name. It made her real. Poor girl! He looked at the heap of dark stones, at the bog, and the dark sea.

'In the war a soldier was lost round here at night. Being a country boy he knew the roots of the heather would tell him where the West was. He heard laughter, by the road here. He crawled closer, saw a group of soldiers with torches, holding Betty between them, having their picture taken.' He looked in front of him, expressionless, savouring the quality of Dougal's attention. 'They must have been strong men. She went softer after she had been exposed to the air.'

He walked on, Dougal keeping up with him, an eager audience. Where a small river came down the hillside he stopped again. 'That's where it crashed. The first German aeroplane shot down in the war. I just happened to be passing. . . .' The story came smooth and polished as a pebble. It may be years, thought Dougal, since he had had someone new to try it on. 'It exploded. The Jerry's head landed just at my feet. Here,' he pointed to his toes. 'I was just thinking, "Well, that's one German less, anyway," when I noticed he hadn't a hair out of

47

place. "By God," I thought, "they must have good hair oil in Germany." ' He cocked his head sideways at Dougal, waiting for his appreciation.

'Thank you for not telling those men where I was.'

'There's many another story of the island. I saw one today. A man inside the stone. You'll be wanting to make a film here, I daresay, and those men were the competition.'

So he had recognised him. 'No.'

'You should.' With no change of tone he said: 'They had guns, I thought. You've not one.' It was not a question. He must have looked Dougal over. He had even caused a collision between them. He really was an old brigand! 'I'm called Abraham Muir. You'll be needing somewhere to stay. We'll see.'

They walked on again, Dougal feeling more cheerful than he had for some time, but also beginning to feel very cold. The wind now carried a sea-fret that wisped inside his clothes, and the rain, which Abraham seemed not to notice, had soaked his trousers to the knee. He confided this to the man, trusting himself to him as to a nanny. Apparently something could be done about his wet clothes as well as about his accommodation. They were in fact approaching some sort of settlement: tiny walled fields surrounded by bog where large, out-of-scale birds with curved beaks picked about like starlings; curlews probably. They rose in flocks and the wind fluffed out their belly-feathers until they looked like the undersides of tabby cats.

'What were you doing on the top of that hill? Do you farm up there?'

'No, no!' He sounded put out at the idea, which, from the unpromising look of the soggy fields, was not surprising. 'I was born there.'

'On the top of the hill?'

Muir looked at him reproachfully. He clearly did not like flippancy in his charges. 'In the village.'

So — here was one of the last children of that empty, beautiful place. . . . A good man to survive with.

Square, comfortless-looking bungalows began to appear along the roadside. A solitary geranium in a garden was fenced on four sides by rattling corrugated iron. The mist turned into thin rain, adding itself to the rain that was already falling. Dougal kept glancing apprehensively at the hill-tops, grateful for the appearance of some shelter, not only from the cold and wet. What he would do if they suddenly appeared, silhouettes on the skyline, he would have to wait and see. He might know his lines when he heard theirs. On the other hand — would they even speak?

Abraham had halted outside an amazing construction: clapboard, the size of a gymnasium. The huge end-walls were curved and moved in and out with the wind, as though the building were a bellows. Steel hawsers held it down. Dougal stared up at it, astounded. 'Put there by the Yanks,' said Abraham. 'They build like that in Alaska.'

Feet apart, Abraham heaved at the door with one hand, holding his cap on with the other. He leaned backwards, the door moved outwards, he managed to pull it open against the wind, a couple of feet, and Dougal, head down, charged towards the gap. As soon as he was inside Abraham twisted round the half-open door, grasped the handle on the inside and tried, unsuccessfully, to prevent the door banging shut, which it did with an explosion that made even him stagger backwards.

When the ripples of that noise died away, and with the sound of the wind no longer in his ears, it was as though a cathedral hush had fallen.

Dotted about the enormous room, quite still — indeed one of them seemed to be asleep — stood several generations of Asians. In front of them, on lines of trestle tables that disappeared into a far-away perspective, was neatly placed every imaginable kind of garment, each one labelled with its price, by hand. There were also long racks of coats, anoraks, trousers. Becoming accustomed to the silence Dougal again heard the wind outside, tearing at the building, and saw the curved end-walls belly in and out like sails.

'They travel the islands' whispered Abraham, who kept close.

'Do they sell much?' asked Dougal, stunned.

'No,' said Abraham, apparently surprised at the question.

They showed no sign of having noticed their entry. *A subject for a romance* thought Dougal, — *in finding a desert city & dwelling there — Asia.* Asia had come to the desert, and forlornly tried to populate it.

Nothing was cheap and everything was shoddy. Shamed, Dougal bought a flimsy pair of overtrousers and the longest scarf they had. It was barely long enought to tie round his neck and when he did so the two ends stuck out like a decorative bow. Abraham pointed out various other articles, as though he was on commision. He probably was, thought Dougal. A large woman in a sari took his money, staring past him, silent.

Outside Dougal tried to digest his incredulity. . . . All that stuff, from island to island, laying it out, packing it up, in this appalling climate.

'We'll see Tommy. About your accommodation,' said Abraham, briskly. Dougal humbly followed, aware that he was entertaining the dotty notion that as long as he was with Abraham he was magically safe. The experience was taking on the unexpectedness of a dream. Apart from anything else, in the drenching rain, Abraham seemed scarcely to get wet.

At Tommy's grocer's shop, on the other side of the little peninsula, the wind appeared to come from the other direction and the door, this time, opened inwards so that they were blown in. Their last arrival had been like a charge of second-row forwards, this one was like the entry of wounded messengers in Shakespeare, all clutch and stagger.

They were received by a long thin man in a white overall, conducted to his parlour, sat in front of a fire and presented, from a tray he reverently brought in, with large goblets two-thirds filled with whisky. He sat and joined them and a conversation took place between him and Abraham. It was in the island monotone, both courteous and evasive, in a manner Dougal had always associated with the Orient. A Widow Strachan was mentioned but after a while, gratefully sipping his whisky, Dougal ceased to listen and contemplated the steam rising from his trousers. He was fairly sure that in Abraham's mind he represented a possible source of revenue for the island — film crews and so on; or, at least, a possible source of further anecdotes.

After a while he found himself being led, by circuitous routes — was Abraham *hiding* him? — to a council house by a Stone Age *broch*. The Widow Strachan fussed over him, presented him with a large fried fish in her hot living-room and conducted him to an upstairs room in which there were many little china ornaments and an enormous high bed. Abraham melted away, leaving the impression that he was easily to be found. The motherly widow also left him, asking him if he would like a fry for his tea.

Dougal took off his wet boots and trousers, leaving them, as instructed, outside his room so that she could dry them in the kitchen, and climbed up into the bed. Warmed, fed, his hands behind his head as he lay back on the large pillows, he listened to the wind and had seldom felt so guiltlessly comfortable.

Brian MacDermott and Jamesy, after examining the cottage, had spent a tiring and unprofitable day. As directed by Abraham they had clambered along the coast in both directions from the bay, in winds that increased, though that had not seemed possible. On the top of a cliff, in the shelter of a rock, they had eaten bread and cheese that Brian had produced from his raincoat pocket. It had been provided by his sister, Jamesy's mother, and was rather stale. However, the older man seemed content, as he ate and then smoked, lying back against the rock. The boy was restless.

'Will he not get away? On the ferry?' he said.

'In this?' said the older man. Below them the sea exploded in columns of white spray, with a noise like heavy gunfire.

51

'It might be calmer on the other side?'

'Climb up on the rock and see.'

Jamesy could barely get a fingerhold and the noise made him dizzy. On top of the rock he could not keep his balance so he lay, shielding his eyes from the tearing air. The sea to the south looked calm enough. A funny colour though, a greeny white. Then he saw a distant freighter, tossed up, apparently balanced and then sucked down. It took a long time to reappear. Jamesy had doubted that it ever would. No small ferry-boat could survive in that. Dazed, he climbed back.

They both lay and listened to the sea. It disappeared into caves far below, crashing and booming and sending up towers of spray, then it sucked itself out in a white boiling. Jamesy shivered. It seemed a terrible place.

'We'll find him,' said Brian. His instinct told him the man would want to meet them; he would know that he could not run forever.

What he would do when they did catch up with him Brian had not yet decided. In a sense, he thought, he was as much on the run as the man he was after. Finbar, one of the men captured because of Dougal's information, was of the younger generation and ruthless in a detached way that Brian had never come across before. Privately, he considered Finbar to be mad, but it takes all sorts to make an army. To protect his own position in the Unit, to block Finbar, it might be necessary to deal harshly with Dougal. Brian was not yet sure. He sighed.

'What shall we do to him when we find him?' asked the boy.

'Shoot him,' said Brian experimentally, and then wished he had not because the boy nodded, and did not seem concerned. 'Your mammy'll be missing you,' he said, thinking of his sister.

'There's no call to talk like that!' said the boy.

'When the time comes, Jamesy, I'll do the talking. And the shooting — if there is any. Remember that.' Brian had faith in his own ability to make decisions but in Jamesy's presence he was uneasy. He had played with the boy, and loved him, since he was born. Such things can cloud the judgement.

Grizelda, in darkness, sat erect in her chair. She was disliking the thought that she has possibly betrayed her son. The words 'betray' and 'son' came to her out of the dark, as abstractions. It was by abstractions that she lived.

Telephoning Lara had partly absolved her, but nothing was to be expected of that drunken, drugged fool. Dougal had married her in order to be envied. 'The most beautiful woman in the world' etc. Grizelda's teeth showed white in the darkness as she smiled. He had had his comeuppance for such vanity. . . . A stinking, American, slut.

She turned over in her mind the possibility of telephoning Elizabeth, Dougal's true wife, but she could not bear the thought of Elizabeth's practical, English voice. Besides, she had behaved grossly. Ten years ago; an ultimatum: she, Elizabeth, could not bear Ireland, its people or its climate, nor could she bear Dougal's work or his theatrical friends. What had she said? 'Dougal was too intelligent to be an actor?' She seemed quite desperate, the silly woman. Anyway, she'd insisted: Dougal must give it all up, come and live in England, on her money, or she would leave him and take the boy.

She had not even had a lover . . .

Odd how people wanted to make an English gentleman out of Dougal. First his father, then Elizabeth.

It must be his obvious lack of imagination.

Of course he refused. But he allowed her to divorce him despite all Father Cuthbertson could say. How he sulked! Went on endlessly, about his son, how he missed him. Had even tried to unburden himself in front of her, one day had even half-cried in her presence — a middle-aged divorcé!

Grizelda was pretty sure he'd refused to go to England with Elizabeth, not from lack of desire, but from lack of capacity. He was afraid of horses and disliked fishing.

He had behaved creditably enough. A cold fish.

Dougal dozed gratefully and was woken by Mrs Strachan with a cup of tea, his dried trousers and boots, and questions about what he would like in his fry. When it was ready she called up the stairs and he descended and ate it while she continually replenished his tea-cup. Afterwards he sat in front of the peat fire in its modern tiled fireplace while Mrs Strachan washed the dishes, talking to him through the open door of the kitchen as she did so, often asking him if he wanted more tea. When she had finished they sat together in front of a small television set and watched a fairly local football match between two teams Dougal had not heard of. Dougal had been vaguely aware of a hum beneath his bedroom window and Mrs Strachan explained that this was her 'Startomatic' generator, she pronounced its name lovingly; it went on when you pressed the first switch of the evening, off when you pressed off the last. Dougal was ashamed he had not noticed her miracle — the possession of electricity on this island — before she had pointed it out to him. He thought of Lara and of how she would have relished Mrs Strachan. First she would have dazzled her and then — here his face fell at the thought of it — she would be bored. He did not seem to dazzle Mrs Strachan. It was as though she considered men babies, in need of spoiling. It might get one down after a bit, he supposed, but it was not an experience he was used to.

After many goodnights and further offers of tea he went upstairs. He found that on one of her numerous quiet errands about the house, unnoticed by him, she had switched on his electric blanket.

In the high bed, Coleridge in hand, monstrously comfortable — the height of the bed off the ground made him feel regal — he set himelf to imagine what might happen to him tomorrow, or within the next few days. He tried to feel fear. It was difficult, in this unlikely house, the 'Startomatic' buzzing below his window. Nevertheless, there were gunmen on the island, who had followed him.

He felt his real besetting fear stir dangerously within him, the one he tried to hide from himself, which was the

54

fear that he had never been able to take anything sufficiently seriously. To some extent, he knew, this had been an infantile reaction against the political seriousness of his mother, which had repelled him.

Had he merely floated through life on his looks, and what he perceived as his charm?

He tried to face the question squarely, frowning, in Mrs Strachan's high bed. Of course he had suffered when Elizabeth had left him. But there had been so many different kinds of pain mixed up in that. Anyway, clearly Liz had detected some lack in him.

He found the memory of that failure so bad that he forced himself to read Coleridge, who seemed to be talking to the point. It was an entry, written in Malta, in which he worried whether the Mediterranean sun might bring all his internal uneases to the surface and make them visible:

'*What if it brought out a deforming eruption on my Face & Body leaving my inner life sound and full of faculty? — O I should rejoice. My Soul she would always love, the faithfully Beloved! and I could more than pardon her aversion for my bodily Presence.*' . . . Could he? Would she? Dougal had found it difficult to show Lara affection since she had begun to smell . . .

Oh Elizabeth, Elizabeth! Why did you leave me? Did you in the end find me hollow? *Am* I? Sitting in bed alone with Coleridge, Dougal at last felt able to let the fear find its form in words.

Afterwards he felt cleansed, like a woman after a tempest of tears. He read on:

'*N.B. to try to understand villains.*'

So Coleridge couldn't, either. . . . That was the trouble: somehow he had to think himself inside the gunmen, and he could not. He had never been able to play such people on stage, never got much beyond narrowing his eyes and curling his lip. He reached for a cigarettte. This time he had to imagine them because he might have to talk them out of whatever it was they intended to do. Would have to *charm* them, dammit, and what's wrong with that? After Malta, Coleridge more or less lived the rest of his life on his charm, and his gab. . . . But Dougal still could not feel his way into men who were able to follow another man, with guns, in order to harm him. How could they care about that abstraction, their cause, so much? Did they have more imagination than he had? Or less?

His eyes still on his book he stubbed out his cigarette in the little flowered saucer by his bed and then, looking at the layers of tobacco smoke that curled around the bedside light, laughed: '*The whole room struck me as Cleanliness quarrelling with Tobacco Ghosts.*' Coleridge was marvellous! . . . '*The plan for one book the Genius of some place appearing in a dream & upbraiding me for omitting him.*'

Dougal watched the layers of smoke settling near the floor and thought of this place: the black and white oyster-catchers, the fluffed-out curlews, the wind. . . . Poor Betty Corrigal's grave, her life, her fate. Such a small transgression. . . . He thought of the old Baron Münchausen who had helped him so much. He was the Genius of this place, and he must not omit *him*. He got up and went to the window. The bedroom light fell on the grassy *broch*. Everything was quiet except for the generator. When he went back to bed and switched off the light it stopped. His had been the last human disturbance of the night. Now he heard the wind again, and the sea.

The two men had returned to the cottage.

When darkness fell the boy made to light the oil-lamp but his uncle stopped him. There was just a chance that their man might risk returning to the cottage if he saw no light. Brian doubted this, but the darkness allowed him peace for his own reflections, protected him from perceiving the restless nerviness of the boy.

Like Grizelda, they sat in the dark.

Like Lara, but not for long. On an impulse she rose, switched on the light and, supporting herself by the wall, made her way to the bathroom. She held her head under the tap and ran a bath. Then she found Dougal's note

56

(under her hair-brush), rang the airport, bathed, rummaged in her disordered cupboards for some clean clothes, pulled them on and, hair stuck damply to her head, left the flat. She had received a sense, the first for a long time, that she was required.

A journalist, hanging around the airport, recognised her, had a chat with the girl at the ticket-desk and then went to the telephone.

5

The next day the wind abated slightly, but there was still no chance of anybody leaving the island. Dougal would not have left, even if he could, because wherever he went afterwards they would have found him. There were teams of highly competitive men paid to tell the world what actors like him were up to, and where, and to make it sound more important than it is.

So he kept himself in view, in the open, visible for miles. Vamping till discovered. . . . He headed towards two long low farms, on a headland. They had a deserted look, as though a light inside their stones had been switched off. As he neared them he saw their roofs were broken, they were blocks of grey, sticking out of cropped grass.

Inside were wooden chairs ranged round the hearth, cupboards, settles, fishing-nets, buoys, kitchen pans, books, half-buried under roof-stones. Outside were ploughs and wooden rollers grown into the turf.

Dougal mourned. There had been no attempt to accommodate to the present. No extensions built on, no patchings with corrugated iron. They had been surrendered; the break with the long past had been total, and brutal.

He wandered to a different sort of desolation. The cropped turf became a broken moor. Miles of bog and oily, iridescent pools and low, wind-bent heather; not even a sheep, and the whole place roared at, resentfully, by the sea. A little headland jutted out from it and on it, incredibly, were the old broken walls of a religious settlement. They were probably Irishmen! To come to this distant island, find its most unpromising spot and then, as though spurning the fleshly temptations of this frightful

59

moor, to build their huts far out in the wild sea! He found it magnificent. Not a denial of a life but a hunger for more. By comparison with such men his own life was puny, and so was the life of everyone he knew.

From places like this they had sailed in little leather boats and civilised the known world — bringing peace, not a sword. But those gunmen who had leaned into Norman's car probably prayed to them. . . . He prayed to them himself; not for his own survival, but for some new sense of significance in the world, and in himself. He was surrounded by abandonments!

'The strongest argument for Xtianity the weak argument that do yet persuade so many to believe — i.e. it fits the human heart.'

You fit the human heart too, STC! That's a great simple statement. It's so often true, that the weak argument is the strongest reason for doing good things.

He stopped. There was a new noise in the air, a sort of underground thunder, and there was some slight, indefinable change in the ground ahead.

He went forward cautiously, testing the ground, and then jumped back in fright. He lay down and crawled forward until he found himself looking down a black hole. At the bottom of it, lightless — he could just see the occasional yellow flash, as though it was showing its teeth — the sea snarled, like a beast in a cage.

The overhang was less on the other side. He felt impelled to see right down into this dreadful place. He picked his way gingerly round it and lay in the heather, his face over the hole. Below his chin it fell away, sheer, as though sawn, black and smooth, into darkness. The noise that came up, echoing, was as though the sea, apparently trapped, bellowed for some prey to be thrown down to it.

Looking sideways, lying flat, he saw how it had been made. The sea had carved a cave into the cliff and here, a hundred yards inland, part of the cave roof had fallen in, leaving this frightful pit.

Something made him look round.

By the abandoned farmhouses were the two men, approaching. Dougal flattened himself further into the heather, his face pointing downwards into the hole. He slightly raised his head and saw the two men had broken into a run, towards him. His mind seemed empty. Then he stood, and ran, heather tearing at his ankles, half-tripping him. He heard a cry and turned. One man stood at the edge of the hole, the slighter, more boyish-looking one, with his arms in the air, balancing, trying to throw himself backwards. While he teetered, shouting, the bulkier man threw himself at him, on the run, in a kind of rugby tackle, to save him. But the young one had already lost his balance and with a scream toppled forward and over, dragging the other man with him.

Dougal stood, alone on the moor. Then he turned and ran blindly, moaning to himself, tearing at his hair, until he was spent. He stopped, hands on knees, grabbing for air. Then he was sick.

There were some newsmen at the airport when Lara landed. She had half-forgotten that her movements could be of interest. She was cheerful with them and then asked for protection, from the airport hotel. She was hurried to the sort of suite she knew well, and detested.

Still, she was feeling pretty good, had drunk nothing on the plane, had only taken a couple of *Serenids*. She took two more and attempted to sleep.

The room, air-conditioned even in this cold climate, had been sprayed with some chemical to remove the fumes of the last occupant, and it reminded her of the life she had married Dougal to escape. She had been doing her best to louse-up that escape and he had gone into a kind of hiding from her a long time ago. True, he had not been quite what she expected. How could he have been, when she could hardly remember what she had wanted? She wanted to see him now, and that was good. It was a double-bed and she pulled one of the pillows toward her, hugging it as she had done when she was a child.

In the morning, as alert as she had been for years — what a ham she was! — there were more reporters and she used her coy husky voice, sipping tomato juice, safe in the knowledge that they couldn't follow her because she had bought all the tickets on the small plane.

'Where are you going, Miss Gray?'

'For a rest.'

Where?'

'I thought you said why?'

'No — '

'Where's Dougal Kerr?' another one interrupted, as she had known someone would. It was easy, she enjoyed it.

'Making some money, I hope.'

She turned from one to another, smiling. She saw them as she used to, acting the part of reporters, her acting the part of the star, and then felt the old, dangerous fatigue.

'Have you plans for a new picture?'

'Look,' she said. She let her jaw go slack and spread her knees wide, like an old woman, so that her skirt rode up. She slumped, round-backed, took a lamp from the bar and held it below her chin at the least becoming lighting-angle. She tried to make herself look as ugly and washed-up as she usually, and on the whole gratefully, felt.

The journalists fell briefly silent, as though abashed.

'You see?' she said, and her flight was called. 'Bye.'

'What'd she do that for?' said one, as they rushed to the ticket office, now they knew her flight.

An older man shrugged: 'She's an actress.'

'She looked a right scrubber.'

'Not to me she didn't, sonny. Whatever it is, she still has oodles.'

'Why'd she flash her knickers though?'

A man behind laughed. 'Wanted a bit I suppose.'

They snarled when they found all the tickets booked and not another plane for six hours. Cursing they moved to the telephones.

At her next stop, shaken by a rough flight in a small aeroplane but also excited by it, she had only local stringers to deal with and they were over-awed. She bought them drinks in the hotel near the harbour, went to the Ladies and left by the back door. In the windswept

62

shopping street she bought herself a pink muffler, yellow gumboots and thick socks, and a dark blue seaman's coat as protection against the astonishing wind. Wearing them, dropping her expensive and unsuitable shoes in a bin, she went by back ways to the harbour. For a moment she stood looking down into the water. There were slivers of oil on it that turned on their sides and swam, like wraith sardines.

A young man in a seaman's cap pottered about in a small launch. He told her it had been a rough night and no one would be going out till the sea settled; though, he said, there was a long way round that was sometimes calmer. She opened her handbag and peered into it. Putting it down on the quay, still open, she crouched and talked more closely to the boatman. Soon he began to laugh, climbed out of his boat, took the money that she handed him and walked along the quay in the direction of other small boats. She went back to the hotel. The stringers were still anxiously waiting, wondering if they dared charge another drink to expenses, and she said she must go upstairs to rest. Glumly, they watched her go.

Around midday the bar filled quickly with the more experienced, more confident men. It was a big story. Lara Gray, alone, on the move at the ends of the earth and apparently planning to go farther. Exasperated, they pumped the local men, who seemed to have discovered nothing. By the time Lara came out of her room they were on the landing, on the stairs, clamouring. Wishing she had Dougal with her, she led them back to the bar. They always liked Dougal. He did tricks with coins which seemed to amuse them.

On her own, downstairs, she flirted, was evasive. One, she noted with pique, but also with sympathy, began to yawn.

At last the young man in the seaman's cap showed at the window and tapped on it. She swung off her bar-stool and the reporters followed. She took a few steps along the quay in her yellow boots and then suddenly jumped into the young man's boat and was caught by him. 'Thank you *kindly*, sir,' she said gaily and he cast off at once, pushing

63

back with his boat-hook one venturesome journalist who attempted to clamber aboard.

'Hey, where are you going, Lara?' 'Hey, Jock, where are you taking the lady?' 'Hey, *McTavish!*'

'We're going a wee trippie roond the aylands, och aye and hoots,' called the boatman, who came from Kent.

Some were already running along the quay to other boats and other boatmen, who all seemed preoccupied. The journalists shouted, argued, the air was full of imprecations. One photographer put down his equipment-bag with such petulance he suddenly feared for it, knelt on the quay and anxiously peered in. As the engine of Lara's boat started, with a belch of water, the journalists jumped into the other boats, and began to argue with whatever boatmen they could see. None seemed willing to embark. Her man had done his job well. She stood by the wheelhouse in her bright scarf, the collar of her seaman's jacket turned up, and called 'Byeee.'

Dougal kept running, whimpering, knowing he could never run from what he had done. Sometimes he stopped, gasping, and tore at his hair with both hands. '*Christ!*'

He asked himself where he was going. Back to Mrs Strachan's he supposed, but what would he think about now as he lay in the high bed! Jesus. It had been so easy. He hadn't even had to think. Maybe they were indeed murderers and had been going to kill him so what he had done was in self-defence? No use. Easy as anything he had led two men down that hole and everything was changed forever.

It was already dark although it was not late. The moor seemed endless. What had that old bastard said — the one who was so easy about poor Betty Corrigal's body, about the brilliantined German's head, about dead people in general? How the lost boy had known where the west was by the roots of the heather? He knelt to look, could discern nothing. Why had he not been taught something useful on those endless hill-tramps at that bloody school? He was kneeling, looking at the heather, when the heavy rain began. He stared down, feeling it almost warm on his neck. What was gone forever was his picture of himself: a man more serious than others supposed (*of course!*) but easy, treading lightly because that way nothing cracks under you.

The ground had cracked under those two, swallowed them. He wandered on, tripping, sometimes up to his knees in bog, half-hoping he would fall down such a hole himself.

Unbidden, a picture came into his mind of his future self; gaunt, silent, a man with a secret; *interesting*. He shook his head wildly from side to side, to cast away the vulgarity of that picture. The devil, friend of frivolity, had sent it. Was trying to make him turn it into a bad play and then he would be truly mad, and damned.

He became aware the moor was ending, but it was not the little settlement that faced him, with its shore-side grocer, the *broch* and the widow Strachan. It was yet another kind of wilderness. The rain poured down his face but the sky was clearer ahead and a shaft of light caught a standing stone, gilding it. Then the sun was obscured again and Dougal, appproaching it, wondered at the stone's strange shape. Sheep grazed round it, and shaggy ponies. He was grateful to be reminded that other creatures existed. He passed other blocks of stone which turned out to be the concrete walls of ruined buildings. One had the words 'Garrison Laundry' written on it in black paint. It was an old camp. And the standing stone, exposed alone in the middle of the green expanse, was a urinal.

Dougal might once have laughed, but the place presented an even deeper desolation than the moor. By the sea were huge piles of rusted armour-plating, all the same dark orange, like certain kinds of lichen; some dreadnought had been dragged from the bottom of the sea. Now the light went out, even from the piles of orange metal, and the heavens opened. Dougal ran desperately for shelter. Two vast Nissen huts faced him, joined together. The words 'Garrison Theatre' on the double semi-circle of the frontage. It was roofless but the foyer remained, behind the frontage was a concrete pillbox and a narrow cubicle marked, just legibly, 'Ticket Office'. Dougal was now very wet and dangerously cold.

The ticket-office was dry enough and had a tiny grate. A broken wooden chair, on a swivel, had a rag of cushion still tied to its seat. Dougal smashed the chair against the floor and the walls, tore the damp cushion into pieces and stuffed some of them into the grate. He felt for matches under his over-trousers, hoping his Asian purchase had kept them dry somehow. They had, just, but their initial reluctance was enough to bring a whimper out of Dougal. He held the barely lit match to the rags which smouldered slightly and went out. His teeth began to chatter. Then the rest of his body began to judder in time with them.

He heard a sound outside, a voice. He crouched in the dark corner, shaking, fearing the whites of his eyes must show, he felt them bulging out of his head. He focused them on a wall and saw an arrow pointing to the open sky above it: 'Dress Circle Bar'.

Two men stood in the narrow doorway, one peering over the other's shoulder. Hatless, their hair was in streaks on their foreheads, their faces white.

'Here's where you are,' said the older man, panting, taking a step into the tiny space. The young man followed him in, with a gun, and said: 'Don't you move now!'

'Put that thing away, Jamesy,' said the older man and the boy lowered the gun but he did not put it back in his pocket. Round the feet of both men puddles gathered on the concrete floor. The boy Dougal recognised as the one who had got him into this mess in the first place. About the older man there was something vaguely familiar.

Dougal began unsteadily to scramble to his feet. 'How did you —'

'Don't move!' yelled the boy at the top of his lungs, aiming the pistol at him with both hands, at arms' length, making a grimace and pulling the trigger. The man knocked his arm up, almost casually, with his elbow, but there was only a click, the gun did not fire.

Dougal was like a crouching statue, one hand on the floor, one leg bent in the act of raising himself. He stayed that way, looking down, breathing heavily.

'Of course it would never fire, Jamesy, after the swim

we've had. And don't do that again, ever. Not till I tell you.' He sounded patient with the boy, but he had authority. Dougal began to breathe more easily. 'Mind if I sit down again?' he said, not moving.

There was no answer, so Dougal, his eyes on the boy, whose teeth were chattering now, slowly subsided back to his original position, his chin on his knees, looking up at them.

With a knife the man began to cut stips of shavings from the chair-leg. He put these in the grate on top of the rags and with Dougal's matches, and some careful blowing, caused a small blaze. The three of them crouched round it.

'We'll be needing some dry clothes,' said the man.

'We could take his,' said the boy.

The man looked Dougal over. That might do it, satisfy Finbar, a public humiliation. The informer left naked on the island.

'They're nearly as wet as yours, dear heart,' said Dougal, showing his trousers, wet to the thigh under the inadequate waterproof pair.

'How did you get out of that hole?' he said.

'Swam,' said the man. 'There was a gap through to the sea.'

'You swam in *that* sea!'

'There was a spit of land,' said the man quietly. 'It sheltered us. There were some walls on it, very old. Old monks. Irish ones I don't doubt. Ireland saved us.' He looked at Dougal. 'How did you get here?'

'It's no distance. I must have walked in circles. I'm glad you fell down that hole.' The man looked at him sharply, his face lit by the fire, some colour returning to it. The boy began to say something, but Dougal over-rode him. '*Other-wise*,' he continued, 'your gun would have gone off and I would be dead.' This time the man looked at the boy. They were like the three witches in *Macbeth*, thought Dougal. 'What would you have done to me if you hadn't . . . lost your footing?'

It was the boy's turn to look at the older man, who stared into the fire thinking that he didn't, himself, fancy a bullet

67

from Finbar. Perhaps it would have been simpler if the boy's gun had worked.

Impatient with his silence, it was the boy who spoke. 'You betrayed four of our best men!' he said.

'*You* betrayed them.'

'I thought we were talking easy — friendly-like,' said the boy, sulkily.

'*Why* — you little whipper-snapper — why did you think that?' He had had enough, and besides, he was beginning to exult. He was not a killer after all. Tragedy was turning into farce. 'Why did you follow me? Why did you want to kill an innocent family?'

'It depends whether you have the faculty of abstract thought,' said the man with infinite weariness, staring into the fire.

Dougal was startled. 'What?'

'You could kill us to save yourself. Just now you tried. Could you sit in an office and plan the killing of a family to save your country — which is infinitely more people than yourself?' His tone was reasonable, patient.

'That was self-defence,' began Dougal.

'Where does that begin, or end?' said the man.

'What is it you want?'

'A united Ireland. I've fought for it. I'll die for it.'

'And cause a family of Germans to die?'

The man looked at him. 'You've not thought about it at all, have you? Not at all, you poor eejut.' He sighed again, and shivered. 'Dry clothes,' he said. 'D'you know where we can find them?'

'Yes,' said Dougal.

Lara was in such bad shape when they reached the jetty that the boatman hesitated to leave her. It had been the worst crossing he remembered, even the long way round, and they had ended up welded together, her arms desperately round his waist while he held grimly onto the wheel.

She did not seem to know where to go, just sat in the pelting rain with her head in her hands. He wanted a rest himself, but he had no intention of going back just yet, in that sea.

He was saved by the appearance of Abraham, descending slowly from the hills. He climbed up and down them often, to observe his old birthplace, and to keep an eye on the comings and goings of the island.

He had his little black Austin 7 parked behind the headland and he sat the willing Lara inside it. 'She'll be all right now, Thomas,' he said to the boatman, who was reluctant to part with her.

'Yes, yes,' came faintly from Lara, from the corner of the back seat. 'I'll be O.K. now. Thanks.' She forced herself to open her eyes in a way that made the boatman beam. 'I feel we know each other *very* well . . .'

After the boatman had returned to his boat Abraham stood for a moment by his car, thinking, oblivious as usual of the heavy rain. That fellow he had walked with yesterday . . . he'd had an air about him. Here was another one. His wife, maybe. Or his mistress. . . . Well, they had their own ways, these people. But they were the sort to make others come to the island. Soon there might be holiday homes, guided tours. Interesting people to talk to.

His mind made up, he climbed awkwardly into the driving seat and turned back, courteously, to his passenger, who had her eyes closed. She was a bonny woman. 'You had a bad crossing the day. You'll be needing a rest. There's a place I could take you to. I took a gentleman there yesterday. Likely you know him?'

'Likely I do,' she said faintly. Then, rousing herself again: 'You're a darling. What do I call you?'

'Abraham.'

'Abraham! What a lovely name! Yes, do take me there darling Abraham. Take me anywhere. But slowly.'

A little flustered by all these endearments Abraham moved off with more of a jerk than he intended and a low moan came from behind him.

Meanwhile the boatman lay on the passenger-bench in the deckhouse of his launch, oilskins folded under his head, thinking of Lara, and the way she had clung to him.

The others would be sure to ask him — Alone with Lara Gray! What was it like, eh? Go on, tell us! But he wouldn't. He could smell her perfume on his jersey now, remember the feel of her cheekbone on his back.

Brian led them surely along the coast back to the little township. He had a better sense of direction than Dougal. They did not speak. The wind was icy through their drenched clothes. When they reached the hole they skirted it carefully.

'It was horrible down there,' said the boy.

'I reckon we're quits,' said Dougal.

'Not yet,' said the other, sulkily.

Dougal, in his physical misery, and in his exhaustion, was suddenly angry. 'Can't you control your youthful companion!' he called out to Brian's back as he plodded on, a few yards ahead.

He showed no sign of having heard. His mouth was set, sometimes he closed his eyes; he was nearly spent. Jamesy could not swim, he had had to drag him from that place. But it was a sense of failure that most exhausted him. They had fallen down that hole through his lack of clear-headedness. Because he had been unable to decide clearly whether he was running after the man who had just outsmarted them (inevitably, in view of his own indecision), or running away from Finbar. . . . He had nearly caused the boy to be drowned.

In the gloom ahead they could see a few small houses straggling, and the huge wooden hut like an aircraft-hangar.

'That's the place,' said Dougal, catching him up, pointing.

Inside it was the same scene that Dougal had come upon the previous evening. The same silent family amid the amazing extent of their wares; the same fat one, heavy-lidded or, in fact, dozing, swaying slightly behind his square yards of socks.

'Anywhere we can change?' said Brian, impatient. A young one gestured with his eyes to the shelter afforded by

70

some cardboard packing-cases. Brian grunted, moving from table to table, selecting two complete sets of garments, tossing one set, piece by piece to his nephew. 'Choose your own suit,' he said to him, picking out a limply-hanging dark blue one for himself. Then he retired behind the packing cases, joined by Jamesy who had chosen a collarless baseball-jacket, red with white stripes, and a pair of jeans. None of the shopkeepers had moved anything but their eyes.

Still concerned with his fate, Dougal strained his ears, but in the creaking silence, amid the shufflings behind the packing-cases, he did not hear them exchange a word.

When they stepped forward the older man was nondescript, with a crispness of lapel and crease that did not look as if it would last long. Jamesy looked as though he should have been leaning against a juke-box.

One of women suddenly moved surprisingly smartly to a till that made bleeping noises as she punched it, scanning them, asking the brand and quality of their underclothes. A man moved behind the packing-cases and stood, looking down; presumably at the sodden piles on the floor.

The bill came to two hundred pounds. 'Oh, and two big plastic bags,' said Brian. The woman pinged her machine again and called in her own language to the man behind the packing-cases who collected the bags and began to shove the wet clothes into them. Brian stepped quickly across to retrieve his overcoat (which, Dougal guessed, contained his gun) and rescued a soggy wallet from his jacket before that was dropped in the bag. From this he extracted a wad of notes, stuck together.

'Wet,' said the woman behind the till, flatly. 'No can take.'

Jamesy grabbed his overcoat from the man and produced his gun. 'Then *we* take!' he said in a high voice.

'*Put that away!*' It was the first time Dougal had heard him raise his voice. The boy, startled, did as he was told. The shopkeepers had shown no reaction. 'It's a toy,' said Brian to the woman. Then he looked at Dougal and raised his eyebrows.

'What was it again?' Dougal said resignedly, producing his damp cheque-book.

'You'll be reimbursed,' said Brian.

'In flowers at my funeral?'

'You'll be reimbursed.'

'When you next rob a bank?'

'Don't push your luck.'

'Oh, go to hell!'

Outside, the two men carrying their plastic bags as though on the way to the launderette, Dougal heard Brian rebuking the younger one. 'Tin-pot gangster . . . offensive weapon . . . they could phone the mainland. . . .' The boy pouted and Dougal began to feel comforted.

Mrs Strachan, as Dougal feared, had another spare room.

'Come in, all of you, you must be starved with the cold. Oh,' she exclaimed at the plastic bags, 'were you caught in that terrible rain?'

'They fell in the sea,' said Dougal cheerfully, while Brian gave him a cool look with his tired eyes.

'Never! Well, you're lucky to be out of it! Now you just go in there and warm yourselves while I pop these in the drier.' She took the plastic bags and bustled off and Dougal heard the 'Startomatic' strike up. They stood, the three of them, in front of the small grate in the front room, in silence.

Mrs Strachan returned and smiled from one to another. To Brian she said; 'Are you in the police-force?'

'No,' said Brian.

'I have a policeman stays here. You have a look of him.'

'Is he here now?' said Dougal,

'No, no. He only comes for his holidays. Will you be taking your tea together, you three men?'

There was a silence. 'I suppose so,' said Dougal.

'You'll be wanting to watch the television,' she said, switching it on. 'And there's yesterday's paper. Falling into the sea! Oh dear, oh dear,' and she went off, shaking her head.

Brian spoke quietly. 'What would you have said to the policeman?'

'Is it your intention to kill me?'

'That was not ordered.'

'Is it your intention?'

'It never was.' It was Finbar I should have killed, Brian thought.

'Why the guns?'

Brian sighed. It wasn't this bollox making a fool of him, it was Finbar, and the confusion he caused. He was a mad-man, the kind the British thought they all were; he was unbalanced, Black and Tan material. The British would have used him and then disowned him. He should have shot Finbar. His father would have.

'We carry them,' he said.

'So — *pax*?' Dougal held his fingers up, crossed.

'This isn't a Public School. . . . We were at school together once.'

'I remember,' said Dougal, wondering if he did.

'We could have shot you at the hole. If we'd wanted to we could have got you.'

'Of course.'

They stared at each other. Mrs Strachan came in bearing the first pot of tea in an enormous cosy. Brian seated himself obediently at the table and tried Dougal's teasing back at him. 'Aren't you coming to join the tea-party?' he said, throwing back his head and examining Dougal along his nose.

'That's jolly decent of you,' said Dougal, seating himself next to him.

Jamesy moved towards the table, his face in the paper, murmuring quietly at the football scores. Closing the paper as he sat down, glancing at the front of it, he suddenly stopped, his mouth open. 'Finbar's out!' he exclaimed.

'Here, let me see that!' said Brian.

A car door slammed, its arrival unheard over the generator and the television, and the doorbell gave its chimes.

6

Jamesy half-sat, half-crouched, on the edge of a camp-bed in a little alcove, his knees almost touching the bottom of Brian's bed.

He was reading the paper, which he had folded longways, to the width of a column, and then lengthways, so that he frowned down at a wad almost obscured by his two thumbs.

Brian sighed. Deirdre had done her best for the boy but whatever could he find that took him so long to decipher in that small area of print? He was good at fixing electrical things, though. . . . But he should never have allowed him into the Unit. That weakness, for Deirdre and for Jamesy, had been the start of the confusion.

Brian had done his share of hard things, of cold watches at street corners, of robberies, of seeing the terror in sometimes innocent eyes, but he had done them clear-headedly, for a soldier must get his hands dirty. But from the moment he knew he must somehow protect Jamesy from the vengeance of Finbar a muddle of motives had led him to an ignominious soaking and to the indignity of tea and rashers with the man he sought.

Jamesy at last turned the paper, settled his thumbs on it again, and began to decipher the other side. If he had looked up at his uncle he would have been startled by his expression.

For Brian was admitting to himself that he was frightened of Finbar in a way that disgusted him, because there was something like superstition in it. There was a madness in Finbar that made Brian's Catholic soul shrink, as though he glimpsed a darkness beyond his imagination. He had even talked to an old priest about him, one who had taught Finbar when he was a boy, and the priest had frightened him still further by looking over and past him, as though withdrawing into some fearful territory known only to his cloth. 'There's a troubled soul,' was all he said.

'Oh, *rubbish*,' Brian swung his legs to the floor.

'What's that, Uncle Brian?' Jamesy looked up, blinking.

' "Brian", Jamesy. Remember? Now we're soldiers together?' He spoke irritably, making the boy stare. 'Have you dried your gun?' He was angling a small electric fire so that it was directed onto the wet banknotes he had carefully separated and laid out, Jamesy watching him. After he had arranged a few more he turned his attention to his gun, dismantling it and laying it beside the banknotes. Then he dried each bullet with his handkerchief and put them to one side. 'See? Now do yours. And finish laying out the notes. First lock the door.'

Jamesy rose obediently and then came back to look at his gun, squinting along the breech under the electric light.

'You're lucky you didn't kill a man with that,' said his uncle.

' "Lucky"!'

'You'd not have been pleased?'

'He was coming at us!'

'Not at all! And what if he was?'

'I've never fired one of these,' said the boy, as though that was explanation enough. His uncle sat in silence, depressed. 'Do we have to give them back, at the English airport?'

'Would you want to fly back to Ireland with the gun in your pocket?' Brian regarded his nephew sadly.

'I bet it can be done.'

'Oh Jamesy, Jamesy!' It came to him, like a temptation, that gaol was the one place where Jamesy might be safe.

The boy had moved on to other things. 'Fancy staying in the same house as Lara Gray!'

'Wasn't she before your time?'

'They show her movies on TV. She's just like them.'

She is indeed, thought Brian, trying to separate more banknotes without letting them disintegrate. Jamesy began an account of the plot of one of her films and he was left to his own thoughts.

Her sudden apparition had disturbed him, had reminded him of his youth and his feelings for Ireland. It was her beauty that had done this, exhausted as she was; her femininity which seemed to embrace and warm them all and yet ask their protection at the same time — for he sensed in her an uncertainty, even a yearning. She made him taste again the passion he had had for Ireland, vowing himself to Her service, yet succoured by Her at the same time. Looking at Lara he had understood how that young pure-heartedness had declined into dogged duty incomprehensible to these people and now not even competent. . . . He had felt tired and jaded, conscious of the absurd tea-party at which she found them, the hunters and the hunted.

Had he been right in sensing that her man had not been wholly pleased to see her? Had recoiled very slightly when she embraced him, her long arms coiled about his neck? He had recovered himself quickly. Then they had been like people in a play.

He probably had another woman somewhere.

They had gone upstairs together, leaving him to ponder what Jamesy had read in the paper.

'It *is* rather narrow,' said Lara.

They stood, arms linked, looking down at the bed. She had kicked off her boots as soon as they came into the room and seemed small, defenceless.

'And high,' said Dougal.

'D'you think we could manage?'

'What do you think?' He tried to keep his eyes from wandering to the Coleridge Notebook by the side of the bed.

'What's that?' said Lara, half-dragging him towards it, flicking the pages. It would have been too brusque he felt,

77

to disengage his arm. He adjusted his balance and stood beside her. '*Think of any number*' she read aloud. It was like her to begin at the beginning, thought Dougal. She was methodical. 'What on earth is it?'

'Coleridge. His Notebook.'

'Why does he put down things like that? I learned it in First Grade.'

'I didn't know you went to school.'

'A woman came to the studio. Why does he?'

'Just wanted to write something, I suppose. Begin the Notebook. Like a pianist, vamping till ready.'

'God, I'm tired!'

'Abraham said it was too rough for any crossing today.'

'He's divine. I think I'll lie down.' She stretched herself on the bed, the pillow pushing her hair onto her cheeks. She looked almost rosy. 'Join me?' she said, pouting, mocking her own pout. How does she manage so many simultaneous expressions, thought Dougal. And each one so slight, as though she lived in close-up. Obediently he lay down beside her, a good part of his back projecting over the floor. She turned his face and kissed him, tenderly.

'It's no good. I'm going to fall off.' He got up, fetched a rickety little chair from the dressing-table and pulled it to the bed. Lara yawned.

'What did you do till you met up with those funny men?'

'I — improvised. Like Coleridge.'

'Did you think they were going to kill you?'

'I wasn't sure.'

'You must have been *terrified*.'

'I was a bit.'

'You poor darling. . . . *How* did you meet them?'

'Well, they rather met *me*. In the middle of a boggy moor. In a disused theatre, actually.'

'On a moor?'

'An old army theatre.'

'What happened then?' Lara was watching him carefully.

'We talked a bit. They had just wanted to scare me I think.'

'Sounds like you gave one of your better performances. All buddies now?'

'Yes.'

There was a small pause. 'Dougal. I *am* pleased to see you.'

'I'm pleased to see you too, Lara.'

She stretched out her hand and linked her fingers with his. 'Are you?' Then she yawned again, smiling. 'God, I really am tired. There were people at the airport.'

'You mean people know you are here?' He should have thought of this.

'Somewhere here. Yes.'

'Then we'd better leave the island pretty quick!'

'Yes,' she said sleepily. Then she opened her eyes. 'Oh God! Why?'

'It might be awkward for those two men.'

'So what?'

'They're not so bad. They make sense, in a way. The older one does.'

'Do they know you feel this way about them?'

'I don't think so.'

'They wouldn't try to kill you tonight, would they?'

'Oh no. The young one's a bit bomb-happy. . . . I'll ask them. Why?'

'They killed people in their beds during Thingymebobs' time. What was his name?'

'Michael Collins. But they were spies.'

'You've been a kind of spy.'

'Not really.'

'I've taken your bed.'

'Oh,' said Dougal, looking at it. 'Well, you need it.'

'They might think I was you.'

Practical Lara. 'I should lock your door.'

'You're laughing at me.'

'Never.'

'What are you going to do?'

'Mm? Well. See the widow Strachan about alternative accommodation I suppose.'

'I feel a beast. There can't be much room left in this house. Full to bursting with your I.R.A. friends.'

'It is rather. I'll have a chat with them, anyway. Make sure I'm not still on the menu. I'll just take Coleridge, if you don't mind.' He carefully leaned over her to reach it. She looked up at him while he did so.

'Dougal. You *are* funny.'

'Am I?'

'This isn't how I imagined it. I think I'll sleep.'

Dougal stood uncertainly in the door. He was letting her down but she had taken him too much by surprise. 'Do,' he said. 'I'll be back.'

He had only gone a few steps down the stairs when he heard her lock the door behind him.

In the kitchen Mrs Strachan appeared a little flustered by the arrival of Lara and at first insisted that Dougal take over the bedroom she had shared with her late husband. Dougal demurred — he did not feel equal to being so unexpectedly at such close quarters with Lara — besides, it put the nice old woman out. At length she agreed to ask among her neighbours and Dougal went with her.

The sound of the front-door closing made Brian move quickly to the window.

'Stay here, Jamesy. Put away your gun. Lock the door behind me. I'll be back soon. And Jamesy — ' he paused at the door, 'those were orders.'

On the dark road along the sea it was easy for Brian to follow the two dim figures, unseen. He did not expect Dougal to call for assistance, but at least he had to make sure he did not.

The two went into a house that looked as though it was still being built. Brian saw the silhouette of a cement-mixer outside it.

Drawing near he saw Dougal and Mrs Strachan under bright strip-lighting talking to a burly man in braces. Dougal was looking round him with a glum expression on his face.

They moved to another room and Brian moved round with them. There were no obvious telephone wires leading to the house. Mrs Strachan came out, holding her little plastic hood to her head and returned to her own house.

Dougal was standing by a small bed that was the only furniture. One illuminated neon strip dangled from the ceiling, partly attached; there was a saw-bench surrounded by saw-dust on the bare concrete floor.

Brian smiled as Dougal flung a book on the bed, sat down beside it, ran his fingers through his hair, shivered, got up suddenly, went to the next room to speak to the man and hurried out of the house. Kerr had seemed very snug at Mrs Strachan's.

He followed him back and looked up at the door, to scare him.

'Just making sure you didn't do anything silly.'

'Such as?'

'Telephoning.'

'I wouldn't do that.' Dougal looked at him in the light from above the door, puzzled. 'It never occurred to me.'

'Why not?'

'The pursued sometimes conceive a strange attraction for the pursuer.'

'Do they indeed.' Letting them both in he called to Mrs Strachan. 'We'll just watch the TV a moment. Is that all right?'

Seated, the instrument drowning their voices from Mrs Strachan, Dougal said, 'You going back to Ireland to bomb more people?'

'Possibly.' Brian sat, impassive, his broad hands on the arm of his chair. He looked rather seedy and poverty-stricken in his new suit. 'Your mother would understand.'

'Pain and grief are the air my mother breathes.'

'Out of each struggle has come a better Ireland.'

'Mightn't things have got better anyway?'

'Perhaps.'

'So — "A Nation Once Again", all problems solved. Any means to be taken to bring that about?'

'It saves lives in the end.'

'Wouldn't the wild men go on making trouble?'

'I can't answer for the other side.'

'Can you answer for your own?'

Dougal, film-actor, trained in *nuances*, felt rather than saw Brian's minute hesitation. The director would have made a quick cutaway, to Brian's expressionless face. 'Oh yes,' was what he said, and went on:

81

'One of the men you put away has gone over the wall. Finbar McLoughlin.'

'A name to conjure with?'

'He won't be fond of you.'

'Or of your nephew.'

'He knows nothing of that. He thinks I gave you the information.'

Dougal stared. He remembered Brian's quick grab at the newspaper, when the boy had exclaimed, just before Lara had come in. He suddenly understood. 'You're afraid of Finbar! That's why you followed me!'

'What I'm telling you is: keep away from Ireland for a while.'

'I've nothing more to fear from you? You won't creep in at the midnight hour and execute me in the name of the Republic? By the way, I won't be in my room. I've moved to — er — superior accommodation. You'll find me next the saw-bench.'

Brian stood up. This mistaken, incomprehensible man made Dougal want to laugh, and also made him dislike himself. Bursts of an idiotic and irritating laughter came from the television. He stood up too. 'I'm sorry,' he said. 'One thing. How did you know I'd come here?'

'Michael Merry suggested you might have.'

'Michael! He knew you were looking for me? And told you?'

Brian regretted the malice that had made him give the name. Dougal's features seemed to have collapsed. 'Yes.'

Dougal looked at the floor.

'You'll keep out of Ireland, then?'

'If you say so.'

'Goodnight, Mrs Strachan. We'll turn off the set,' Brian called. She came in drying her hands. 'You'll not have a pot of tea? Or a hot drink?' 'I'll just go up and speak to my wife.'

Brian led the way upstairs, stopped at his own door and knocked. 'It's me, Jamesy.' The door was unlocked and he went inside.

Dougal stood alone outside Lara's door. *Michael Merry*. . . . Oh Dougal Kerr, Dougal Kerr, what sort of a man are you to have gone through life without making one loyal friend?. . . He tried the doorknob of Lara's room but it was locked. He called softly. There was no reply. He turned, went down the stairs, and after one more encounter with the lurking Mrs Strachan, left the house.

There was a wind, of course, and it was cold. He turned up his collar. There was a feeling like a bruise, somewhere under his breastbone, a sense of nausea.

His host, rather blood-shot after what was doubtless a long evening's do-it-yourself, was measuring up some window-fittings in his windowless sitting-room — where did the man sleep? — and after being let in Dougal went to his room.

It was arctically cold, and dazzling in the shadowless light of the dangling neon tube. He looked grimly at his bed.

There was no chance he could get out of his clothes. He saw his breath going up in clouds. And his tooth-brush was locked in with Lara . . .

Taking off his shoes he climbed between the sheets, smelling the blankets as he did so. The lump on top of him was Coleridge. He reached for the book and held it above him, feeling his hands go numb with cold. Coleridge had hit a dull patch, descriptions of Malta, little scratched drawings, etc. He was trying to keep himself occupied. Then Dougal laughed:

'*The dread of mind that the possibility of my feeling the Spirit of the Ludicrous while a great man is talking to me with holy passion.*'

He had felt everything! Had met Brian MacDermott.

Then he remembered the light and knew he could not get out of bed into that icy air. If the man had one of those generator things it would presumably go out when he himself went to bed. Dougal put the Coleridge under the bed-clothes with him, like a teddy bear. He pulled them over his head and tried to breathe through his mouth, to make a pocket of warm air and also to prevent his smelling the blankets, and curled round the hard corners of the Coleridge.

It was like a burden lifted: Brian MacDermott had taken a decision and found his mind working properly again.

83

When he got back to Dublin he would return Jamesy to Deirdre and that was that. The boy was no use for the work and his mother must accept it. Family feelings had disturbed his judgement. Now he could feel it moving with its old, pleasurable logic.

It would mean the end of a goodish period. Childless, unmarried, Brian had been taking Jamesy off his mother's hands since he was three or four years old. Deirdre had five more and two were younger than Jamesy. Slowly he had discoved how much he enjoyed the child's company, and what they did together: going to railway stations to watch the trains, slow walks through the city streets.

He had come to depend on it. There was not much happening otherwise. In those days there was little sympathy for the Army underground. They were either feared, as fanatics likely to disturb Ireland's new-found comfort, or laughed at as out-of-date, fighting old battles; indeed, there was an element of home-spun and hurley among some of their supporters. But Brian was a professional, in non-active circumstances, and he made sure that a chain of command was kept in readiness, and well-kept weapons hidden. Since 1969 and the troubles in the North the membership had grown immeasurably. As usual, the behaviour of the British did their recruiting for them. That there had been anything at all for the new activists to turn to was, he knew, largely owing to him and a few colleagues. Nevertheless, it had been a lonely time, demanding perseverance and cunning, and with Jamesy he had been able to relax and be simple.

He had not had a long childhood himself. His father had been on the run, moving from house to house, shot in the end by Irish Free State troopers. He would not agree to the oath to King George. The oath which just fell away, was forgotten, but before that was the cause of the death of many Irishmen, at the hands of their kindred. . . . Republicans like his father were considered hot-heads, likely to endanger the chance of a fruitful peace.

But he had decided to kill Finbar because he was a threat to future peace . . .

84

The circumstances were not the same! The campaign had to be controlled. Finbar pursued personal vendettas. He had disobeyed orders, pulled off strikes which were so successful that their lack of authorisation was fudged over. Nevertheless, he was out of control, a danger to the future. He, Brian, would take responsibility for removing him. That man downstairs was right. He had been afraid . . .

That was a clever trick leading them into the hole. Perhaps he had not known he was doing so. . . . Acted instinctively. Brian remembered thinking, as he went over, 'This is what comes of not making up your bloody mind!' It wasn't so deep, thank God! The water was terrible. But luck had held. It would hold in Ireland too. Or it would not. No man's luck lasts forever. At least Jamesy would be out of it.

So would Finbar, Brian thought before he slept. Plenty of time, though. The paper said he had dived off the prison ship through the barbed wire in the water. He would be a mess for a while. It was a splendid thing to do. But they were not in the splendour business.

Brian, the professional, thought of Finbar in much the same way as Michael Merry thought of Dougal.

In the morning they all sat round one of Mrs Strachan's huge breakfasts, Lara disappointing her by only crumbling a piece of toast and Dougal worrying her by looking unusually seedy. He assured her that he had been perfectly comfortable but when she was out of the room he explained to the rest of them his need to pull his wet trouser-legs away from his shins. Finding a basin in the half-made house he had filled it with water, washing, and pulled out the plug. It had been unattached to a waste-pipe.

Only Lara laughed.

Dougal sensed that Brian registered disapproval of his smarty-pants derision of poorer people's plumbing arrangements and so could not resist goading him. 'Extraordinary, the amount of farce that surrounds us. What the British police call "The Paddy Factor". I think I'll go and brush my teeth in your room, Lara.'

Brian watched him leave, with a heavy expression. The sooner this trip was behind him the better.

Lara, in a cream silk blouse and a grey tweed skirt, seemed to him altogether extraordinary. He knew of course that she was invested for him with the glamour of some of the parts he had seen her play, but it was more than that. Her man was no good at all. Content to portray the kind of Englishman Brian and the rest of the world most mistrusted, with an inch of white cuff and a boyish grin. But Lara Gray ... her thin wrist with a single heavy bracelet on it, the white fingers breaking the toast against her plate, her loose hair, her eyes. It was as though she had known suffering, known warmth and forgiveness. He allowed her to help him remember — no, to reinhabit! — all that was best in himself; remember the reason for his boyhood vow to Ireland. She might be nothing herself, but no matter; she reminded him of his faith; he saluted her for what she was: a Muse.

Meanwhile Dougal looked round his old room as he gratefully brushed his teeth and noted how completely Lara had taken it over: her pots and tissues and clothes were everywhere. Well — at least she'd begun to make an effort and didn't smell so bad. She seemed to be rather enjoying herself. He wondered how long it would last and guessed, bleakly, that it rather depended on him. But how? He'd tried everything — amorousness, indifference, tyranny. *Anything*, to bring the life back into her face. But nothing worked for long. The look of disappointment and withdrawal came back.

Shaving, he looked at his own face in the mirror. The face of a man who did not love his wife, whose friends shopped him at the first opportunity, whose life so far seemed to have been wasted, who could find no interest in any probable or possible future. Yet he looked quite cheerful. Even felt it. He was even rather enjoying the after-taste of the toothpaste, for God's sake! What a very little we need to keep us going. On the other hand, what a mysterious amount Lara seemed to need.

He stood in front of the electric fire and tried to dry his trousers without setting them on fire. He stared down into the fisherman's bag Norman had lent him. He had taken

86

his spongebag from it but had not noticed the half-bottle of whisky was gone. No wonder Lara had slept so sound, had not heard his knock. He looked round the room for it. No sign. God, don't say she's started to hide the empties ...

It had been arranged by Mrs Strachan that Abraham should come in his own car, accompanied by a taxi, to take them to the ferry. Dougal had insisted on the second car, had not fancied the idea of squeezing into one car with his pursuers — the last touch of farce. He looked out of the window at the sea. Hard to tell, but it did not look *too* rough. He heard the chime of the doorbell, and then, with pleasure, Abraham's voice, high and slow, in the hall. Picking up the fisherman's bag, switching off the fire and creating the stillness behind the house that filled him, already, with nostalgia, he went down the stairs, his trousers now warmly damp instead of coldly so.

Abraham was dressed in the same clothes he had been wearing when they met. Mrs Strachan, spots of colour in her cheeks, was deep in intimate and excited conversation with Lara. The two gunmen stood. Dougal had time to think, with surprise, that Lara had a talent for turning herself into a daughter, and to wonder if there was a clue for him there, before Lara broke off, saying she must run upstairs to pack.

Dougal settled his bill, which was small, and told the widow Strachan he would like to spend the rest of his life with her. Her delight made Brian grunt, as though he suspected Dougal of turning on the patronising Ascendancy charm, but there were few things he had ever said, Dougal thought, that were more true.

'I see you met up with your friends, then,' said Abraham.

'You know each other?' said Brian.

'Oh yes,' said Abraham.

'Two cars?' said Dougal. He really cared about this last touch.

'Oh yes,' said Abraham.

Brian, fumbling in his pockets, produced a pile of crinkled notes and some change. He offered them to Dougal. 'I think you'll find that's right.'

'Thank you,' said Dougal, surprised. 'I'm relieved you're back in your old togs though.'

Brian said nothing and Abraham was looking from one to the other with obvious amusement. 'I see you've made up your differences.'

Lara was coming down the stairs with her bag. 'You know this divine man?' she said, to Dougal.

'We're old friends,' he said.

'We are,' said Abraham. 'I met him hiding in a grave,' and his shoulders began to shake.

'So!' said Brian, quietly.

They drove along the coast in convoy, Abraham driving Dougal and Lara, and, mindful of Dougal's presence, giving Lara abbreviated versions of his Betty Corrigal and German airman stories. Dougal was surprised that he did not repeat them word for word.

Then they stood, the five of them, in the usual wind, waiting for the ferry.

'I'm scared, said Lara, shivering.

'It won't be too rough today. Look at it.' He meant to draw her attention to the approaching ferry, and how crowded it was. Then he saw it was crowded indeed, but with an unlikely bunch of passengers. Journalists. . . . Some of whom looked in considerable distress.

Quickly Dougal pulled them all behind the rock that overlooked the jetty. 'Abraham. Those are reporters. They want to interview my wife, she's an actress.'

'I know,' said Abraham.

'Take them to Betty Corrigal's grave, and the place where the German crashed. The island's better copy for them, they'll love it.'

'They've not come before because of an industrial dispute among the ferrymen,' he said slowly. 'I never heard of such a thing.' He was at his most inscrutable, looking at Lara. 'Maybe the lady spoke a word or two, not wanting to be disturbed.'

'Will you help us, Abraham?' She smiled at him, full voltage.

'I will,' he answered at once, almost fervently. 'Will you

be coming back to the island?'

He addressed the question to her, but it was Dougal who answered: 'Abraham, if I have a wish in the world, it's that.'

'It's a grand place for the tourism,' said Abraham, nodding, as though a bargain had been struck.

'Look,' said Dougal urgently, 'They're landing.' Some were holding on to each other, others were more sprightly. Two figures detached themselves and stood apart, uncertainly. No one had seen the group behind the rock. Abraham approached the reporters with deliberation.

'It was a lousy trick to throw Abraham to that lot!' said Lara. 'They'll flay him.'

'They'll love him,' said Dougal. 'He'll wake up a star. They've got to send *some* copy back, poor sods! Look, he's hypnotising them. Let's run for it.'

As they ran they had to pass the two separate figures, who turned. One was Norman Cudforth. The other was Michael Merry.

'Dougal!' Merry called out as they approached.

'Hallo, Norman' said Dougal, panting. 'Where's Mary?'

'Gone home,' said Norman bleakly, staring first at the gunmen, then at Dougal and Lara. 'Excitement too much for her.'

'Dougal, my dear old boy!' called Merry. 'And Lara! You both look marvellous.'

'Must fly,' said Dougal.

'Just thought I'd like a glimpse of Norman's famous island. Vultures gathering? *Must* you go?' His eyes moved towards Brian but Merry gave no sign of recognising him.

One journalist began to walk towards them. They turned quickly towards the ferry and ran on, Brian and Jamesy leading.

Dougal caught up with Brian. 'That the fellow who told you where I was?'

'He'd no reason to think we meant you harm.'

'Did you?'

'You caught me at a rare moment of indecision,' said Brian, smiling, exhilarated to feel the planks of the ferry-deck at last under his feet.

89

'May there be many more of them,' said Dougal, helping Lara aboard.

'Oh I don't know,' said Brian. 'They can be dangerous.'

The ferryman, Lara's friend of the day before, had not switched off his engine and now cast off as soon as they were all aboard. The group around Abraham turned as the engine noise grew louder, and there was a shout, but Abraham must have continued talking, and promised them something interesting, for they turned back to him. Dougal wondered what it could be. Lara kept herself out of sight, in the wheelhouse.

Dougal stood looking back at the island until the little concrete jetty merged into the coastline and he could see nearly the whole length of the road he had walked with Abraham, after he had laid hidden in the tomb. He was a sort of Lazarus, he thought; without conviction.

'It was damn cosy at the Widow Strachan's,' he said, to the island.

Lara, unnoticed by him, had come out of the deckhouse and stood by him, clutching the side of the boat as it lurched.

'I didn't notice,' she said softly, almost in his ear, so that he felt her breath. 'I was too drunk.' She looked at him from below her brows, in a way that made his stomach lurch, though it might have been the action of the ship. 'I didn't think that bed was too damn narrow either.'

7

At the airport on the mainland they handed back their guns to the contact who had provided them.

He was an Englishman — at least to Brian he was, if not to himself — whom Brian did not know. He was flashily proud of the secret compartment behind the car radio where he put the guns.

'Job finished?' he said.

Brian looked at him.

'Good.' The man leaned against his car in the airport car park and adjusted the wing-mirror so hc could see behind them. Bloody fool, thought Brian. If anyone had been vaguely noticing them he would be interested now. 'Didn't see anything about it in the papers.'

Again Brian said nothing, his head bent slightly forward, looking upwards at the man, thinking: You're suspiciously free and easy with your superior officer, Jacko. What's been going on?

'D'you hear Finbar was out?' said the man, looking down at his nails, picking them.

It's George Raft is your model then? And you Finbar's man? Brian's continuing silence seemed to rattle him. He jerked alive when a car parked near them and called out, to Brian and Jamesy: 'The four gross you ordered'll be on their way tomorrow. I've rung head office. It's been a pleasure doing business with you. Cheers. Go carefully now,' and got back into his car.

He watched Brian and the boy disappear into the airport building, waited a few moments, then he got out of his car and went in by a different entrance. After looking round, he went to the telephone. From the balcony above the main concourse Brian watched him.

At Dublin airport they bumped into a young man who acted surprise at seeing them. 'Go all right?'

'What did?' said Brian. This fellow was not meant to know anything.

'Oh, we guessed you were onto something. Find the actor-fellow?'

'We did.'

'That's all right then. Finbar'll be pleased about that.'

'I daresay.'

'Going home, now are you?'

Brian nodded slowly, examining the young man. A lot seemed to have happened in the last few days. He had better go carefully. 'Something like that,' he said.

They took a taxi. At traffic-lights by the Canal he paid off the driver and climbed out, pulling Jamesy behind him, into the small streets.

'Where are we going?'

'To your Mam's. But first I've a call to make. Stand just here and take notice of anyone who passes.' He pressed the latch of a gate in a high brick wall and disappeared. He was gone a few moments and the only passer-by was a woman wheeling some groceries. When he returned Jamesy noticed the slight bulge in his pocket.

'You've got a gun!'

'I think we were followed from the airport. By MacDaid.'

'But he's one of us! Why should he do that?'

'Finbar's a funny man.'

'Where are we going now?'

'I told you. To your Mam's. Come on now, don't keep looking back, we're on our own.'

'But the Unit wouldn't let Finbar hurt you?' Jamesy was appalled.

'Not at all! It's all politics, Jamesy. Don't bother your head about it.' Brian laughed, to cheer him. So woebegone did Jamesy look that Brian, nearly forgetting the passage of the years, felt tempted to take his hand.

At the house Deirdre was berating one son for not getting down to his homework, another for bringing his bicycle into the house and an older daughter for sitting painting her toe-nails when there was clearing up to be done. Meanwhile she piled plates from their tea and took them to the sink.

After she was over her relief at seeing Jamesy safe — yet she wants him to be with the Unit, thought Brian — he suggested, gently, that he would like to have words with her alone. Frowning slightly, drying her hands on her apron, she gave a despairing glance round the room, recognising the impossibility of clearing it of children. She led Brian up to her bedroom. She stood uneasily by the little empty fireplace, a coloured picture of the Sacred Heart, His hand raised in blessing, on the wall behind her. Brian sat uncomfortably on the edge of the bed that nearly filled the room.

'It's about Jamesy, Deirdre. He's not quite ready for the Unit.'

She drew in her breath. 'He's done something wrong!'

'No. It's not that.'

'Then why? He's safe with you. Otherwise he'll go off and do something of his own.'

'We both had a hand in that — telling him stories.'

'But they were true!'

'Of course they were.'

'What, then?'

'It's the work. He's not suited.'

'You think he's stupid!'

'No — he's a good boy.' He sat himself more upright on the bed. 'He admires his grandfather. Now, say his grandfather had belonged to a regular army — like the German one, or the British. He would like his grandson to be a soldier. So he joins up, and all sorts of people, sergeants, officers, watch him and report on him. They decide whether he will make a soldier or not. There's no disgrace if they decide not. Well, we're not an army like that but I'm his sergeant, his officers, rolled into one. And that's how I'm reporting.'

'You think he won't do?'

'Not yet, Deirdre.'

'God, it'll break his heart'

'There are other considerations.'

'Such as?'

'I've been around a long time.'

'You're not thinking of giving up?'

'They might have me out.'

'*You?*'

'In one of those regular armies they might shunt me off to command a depot or something. They might even do that in this case, I don't know. Besides,' the time had come to appeal to her directly, 'I can't be Jamesy's uncle and his officer at the same time.'

She saw that. He had known she would. A military expression settled on her face, replacing the indignation. 'Have you told him?'

'I thought I'd tell you first.'

She went to the head of the stairs and called Jamesy up, gentleness in her voice. Brian prepared himself for the moment. Love and war did not mix. He said a prayer to the picture on the wall, with the unmoving gestures of blessing and peace, that he might find the right words and not hurt Jamesy too much. He heard him coming up the stairs. 'What is it, Mam?' The boy stood in front of him, his mother behind his shoulder.

Brian shifted along the bed and patted a place beside him. The boy sat next to him, wondering.

'That was good trip we had, wasn't it, Jamesy?'

'It was!' The boy was fervent.

'Well, as your officer I was watching you, seeing how you shaped. You did well — promising — but I don't think you're quite ready to be a full member of the Unit. Not just yet.'

'What'd I do wrong?' The boy looked from Brian to his mother and back again.

He appeared to have forgotten he had caused four of their men to be caught. Brian went on, with new confidence. 'Little things, none of them important, but they showed you might be useful to the Unit in other ways, later.'

94

'But what *were* those things?'

'You shouldn't have pulled your gun on that man, not without —

'You showed him the gun, Jamesy?' Deirdre sounded proud.

You foolish woman, thought Brian, sighing. Foolish in that way, anyway.

'He was going for his own. He'd nearly killed us anyway.'

'Oh Jamesy!' Now she was upset, at the thought of the boy in danger, and Brian began to lose patience with her — what sort of a game did she think all this was? — which made it easier to be firm with Jamesy.

'You were acting against orders.'

'Just for that you'd throw me out?'

'Yes, just for that, Jamesy.' He put out his hand to touch the boy, but he moved away, stood up.

'Well, that's that then. I'll be downstairs, Mam.' Dignified, he left the room.

Brother and sister were left alone, in silence.

'Deirdre,' said Brian, heavily, 'I'd love a wash.'

'You'd better do it in the hall. The bathroom's a hell of a mess.'

He followed her down the stairs, fearful of having to face Jamesy again. But the narrow passage to the front door was empty, blocked by a bicycle.

'They get stolen round here,' said his sister. 'I've bought Declan a padlock but he says they know how to pick it. The neighbourhood's going down.'

It had been going down ever since Brian remembered. He felt a movement of warmth towards his sister. She'd had a hard battle since her man died.

It was cramped in the little lavatory under the stairs as Brian bent over the basin, and his gun felt heavy in his pocket. There was nowhere to hang his jacket so he went into the passage and hung it among the macintoshes and anoraks. Rolling up his sleeves, filling the basin with cold water, he immersed his face in it for as long as he could and then, spluttering, pummelled his face with the towel.

95

He had a feeling he might need a clear head within the next few hours.

Well, he was rid of Jamesy. Nothing would be quite the same between them ever again. But he could now think properly.

He examined his face in the mirror, blotched red and white by the rubbing. He felt lonely. The sooner he reached some allies the better. He would tell them what was in his mind about Finbar. It would come as no surprise to them. What amateurs the others were! That fellow in England, leaning against his car, playing at gangsters. "The Paddy Factor". . .

In the hall he reached up for his coat as Jamesy came out of the kitchen.

'I'm sorry, Jamesy. We're still friends, aren't we?'

'It's because I blabbed, isn't it?'

'We'll talk about it in six months.'

'*Six months*!' To the boy it sounded like eternity.

Brian was now outside the front door, looking about, Jamesy following him. At the top of the steps, to soften his departure, though he was desperate to be off, he turned: 'I must go. A meeting. Top-level stuff. . . .' After the absurd phrase he ran down the steps onto the littered street leaving Jamesy outside the front door. He did not look back.

A car pulled up to the kerb and stopped in front of him. He had not seen it approach, he had been turned to Jamesy.

Finbar, in the passenger seat, bandaged hands in his lap, said: 'Get in, Brian.'

Brian's hand went to his pocket. It was empty. Jamesy! . . .

'I shouldn't try that,' said a man in the back, a gun in his hand.

'Get in,' said Finbar, quietly.

Brian thought of making a dash back to the house. Jamesy, his mouth open, stood in the way. If they opened up they would get Jamesy. 'Sure,' said Brian. 'Kind of you. Good to see you, Finbar.' Opening the back door he settled himself inside.

'Brian!' he heard Jamesy's alarmed cry, and felt his companion's gun in his side.

The boy's white face was at the car window. 'Hallo, Jamesy,' said Finbar.

'Where are you all going?' The boy's eyes travelled round the inside of the car.

'Top-level stuff,' said Brian, from the back seat.

'That's right,' said Finbar, nudging the driver with his elbow, his eyes on Jamesy. The car drew away leaving Jamesy staring after it.

'The boy had a gun,' said Finbar, to nobody in particular. 'Your body-guard, Brian?' he laughed. 'What a pair!'

Two old hands had not travelled to the island with the rest of the reporters. Partly through weight of years, and influence with their editors, partly because they knew that making yourself uncomfortable did not necessarily make you a good journalist, they stayed where they were, near telephones, in a comfortable bar. As a result they had Lara and Dougal to themselves.

Dougal they knew, he was almost an old friend, but Lara's reputation had been made in America and as a result she bewitched them. Dougal to them was the home counties, Elstree, Denham. But Lara was Hollywood.

They sat at the bar and played liar-dice, the four of them, and Dougal did his tricks with coins which they had seen before but did not mind because he knew when to stop. Lara was a revelation, turning their questions into conversation, companionable, easy — one of the boys — which she so evidently and beautifully was not. They became four friends of passage, who happened to find themselves together in a hotel in a lonely place. The story seemed straightforward enough: Dougal had slipped away to the island to rest and 'do a bit of writing' — he had remembered that most ageing actors said that nowadays. Lara had followed discreetly, hoping not to be noticed.

Yet, their noses told them there was something not quite right about the story. Why had they left the island so soon?

Who were the two men they had disembarked with, who disappeared so quickly? Dougal said they were people they had met on the ferry. Perhaps. They hadn't *looked* like that.

The two journalists drank too much, partly out of habit, partly to encourage Dougal and Lara to do the same. They were not successful in this, which made them watchful.

After lunch, and more drinking by the journalists, Lara and Dougal went to their room and the newspapermen settled down to wait for the return of their stranded colleagues. They might come back with something.

Lara had a bath, to Dougal's relief. It seemed to inaugurate a new era. These last few days had made her positively rosy. He had a bath after her, to wash off the smell of the previous night's blankets, but she had not left much hot water.

When he came out of the tiny bathroom, a very small hotel towel wrapped round his middle, she was lying on one of the single beds in her petticoat. He noticed how pretty her bare feet were and remembered that he had always admired them, although he had not dared look at them for ages. He hadn't looked at *her* for ages. While he was doing so, hesitating — her eyes were closed — she surprised him by saying softly: 'This bed's pretty narrow too.'

'Oh, I don't know . . .'

She sat up, pulled her knees to her chin, modestly wrapping the skirt of her petticoat round her shins and, with a look of such warm affection that Dougal was further stirred, said: 'What are we going to do?'

As he moved towards her she said: 'Do we go back to Dublin?'

'Oh. I see,' said Dougal, halting. 'I'm not sure.'

'What d'you mean "not sure"?'

'Brian MacDermott rather suggested –'

'Was that his name? You *were* pally!'

'He thought it would be a good idea if we didn't. For a while.'

'Because he'd get you there?'

'No, no. One of the chaps they captured has escaped. Brian seemed to think he might hold his arrest against me. Sounded a bit scared of him himself.'

'That settles it. I was bored with Dublin anyway.'

'No!' Dougal was pleading. 'Not leave Dublin for good! I can't bear the thought of living in England.'

'I know Elizabeth and the boy are there. But we've got to sort all that out one day, haven't we? Meanwhile we've got to find somewhere to go. O.K.?'

'O.K.'

Lara straightened her back suddenly. 'Billy Binkley!'

'Christ!'

'No, listen. He's got this place in England. He's always telling me to borrow it. Keeps it fully staffed, deep in the Surrey woods. He's in California. They'd never find us there, the Press, the Irish, nobody.'

'You make Surrey sound like Sherwood Forest.'

'He hid Cary there when he was shooting in England. And Liz.' She paused. 'Though I don't think anyone tried very hard to find her.'

'Did he really?' Dougal was impressed. 'But, God, it'll be fake Old Masters, fake patios, ten swimming pools, fake Great Danes . . .'

'So what? It's not for long. Besides,' she looked intently at him, 'we'd be together.'

'That'd be the best part.'

'I'll ring him.' She was decisive.

'In California?'

'Sure.'

'From *here*?'

'Do the telephones work by gas or something? Why not?'

'Well — what about the time difference?'

'He'll be in the jacuzzi about now. Or up to no good. Which reminds me,' her voice changed, she looked at him with soft eyes. 'All that doesn't matter.'

Dougal was tempted to ask 'All what?' but he knew what she meant and her understanding tone rattled him. With what dignity he could he lay on his own bed while she busied herself happily with the telephone at her bedside. There seemed to be some difficulty.

'She's gone to get the goddam manager,' said Lara, lying back. A pause, more conversation, Lara growing incredulous. Then she put down the receiver and lit a cigarette.

'Would you believe it? They want a deposit before they'll book the call!'

'I can believe it very easily.'

'Would you be an angel?. . .'

'Mm? Oh. All right.' Dougal got up rather sulkily and dressed.

Downstairs, on his way to the manager's cubby-hole he passed the bar, surprised to see the two journalists still there, drinking alone.

'You *bastard*!' said one of them, with real venom.

Dougal stopped, and a copy of the local paper, just off the press, was pushed at him:

'FAMOUS STAR IN REAL-LIFE DRAMA. Dougal Carr' — Dougal grunted — 'firm-jawed hero of so many films and TV shows (viewers will remember him as the lady-chasing, fox-hunting squire in the "Manners Makyth Man" series)' — Dougal exclaimed, in pain: 'God, that wasn't me! That was Michael Merry!'— 'yesterday, in true Sir Joshua fashion, outwitted two dangerous IRA gunmen by leading them a wild-goose-chase across bags until they fell into the sea. After swimming in rough seas to rescue them he bought them new clothes and paid for their accommodation at one of the best hotels on the island. With the churm that so many leading-ladies have found irresistible, he and the gunmen became fast friends. In an exclusive interview with ex-postmaster Abraham Moat . . .'

'Across *bags*!' said Dougal.

'Cut out the churm,' said the man, not smiling. 'You said there was no story.'

'They didn't even spell my name right. That old man made it up.'

'Who were the men who got off the boat with you?' They closed round him, half-threatening, half-beseeching.

They would crucify him, for years, if he didn't give them something.

'Oh *hell*,' he said.

100

They crooked fingers at him, beckoning, pointing to a chair at the table. 'Tell Daddy.'

'I must just see the manager.'

'We'll come with you. Then we'll have a nice, long chat.'

'Since the time of Queen Elizabeth our people have been murdered, starved, suppppressed. Englishmen have tried to take our religion from us, our language from us. They have taken from us the produce of our lands and the work of our hands. Ships have left Ireland laden with good things for England while the people who made those things, who grew those things, were left to starve. Not left in peace even to die. When they huddled in their poor dwellings, the very roofs over their heads were ripped off — by the English, who else but by the English and the servants of the English? — and they were driven into the lanes to die there. We all know the long, terrible story. And it is true. Terribly true.'

Grizelda, her chin thrown back, the hollows in her face made more skull-like by the overhead lights, was telling the story that never failed to move her, and never would fail. 'But we have fought! We have suffered, endured, tried every possible peaceful means to obtain justice, simple justice, but when the suffering became *un*endurable, when we were pushed *beyond* endurance — and Oh! how often did that happen! — we have *fought*. Because never, in the lowest depth of our humiliations, did we cease to be the "indomitable Irishry".'

The white heads, and the bald heads, seated round the table in the large hall, nodded and banged their cutlery. Veterans of the Rising in Easter 1916 — the few of them still left — and of the Troubles, and of the Civil War after the Treaty, it was what they believed, their common ground, and what they had come to hear said again. For it was true.

'And *how* have we fought?' Grizelda's voice rose. 'With bare hands, with pitchforks. Then, of course, we were called a Mob. So we dressed in uniforms, in 1916. I see

101

some here who well remember that time, fewer this year than last, but you will never be forgotten. We declared a Republic. The might of the English army was turned on us. We expected that! We surrendered, according to the forms of War. And what happened then. We were shot, behind closed doors, after secret trials that were no trial. Day after day a trickle of blood flowed under the door England had slammed on our heroes. We were not a Mob now. We were in uniform, so now we were called clowns. We took to the hedges and ditches, rifles and pistols against armoured cars and machine-guns, manned by the dregs of British prisons. Now we were called murderers!

'They will never learn! Still we fight, and still we are called murderers! And still our people are *oppressed*!' She banged the table on the last word, knowing that a slow degeneration, of age or of complacency, had taken place in some of her audience. Faint hearts! 'I know there are some here who are uneasy, who do not like what is happening today. Who could like it? But our brothers and sisters in the Six Counties do not feel that way. They live in terror of their own police. Terror for their lives, their property. Is that civilisation? Is that a civilised country under the beautiful benefits of the British Crown? No! It is barbarism! The Dark Ages! And if our methods seem barbaric what others are there, in the face of barbarism! We must *hate* what is wicked! Hate! Hate! Hate! For hatred gives us energy and strength. We must hate so that we may have the opportunity to love. We must force the last English boot off our soil so that Ireland, the Ireland of our hearts' blood, the Ireland of our love, shall at last be born!'

Amid the table-thumping and clapping some glances were exchanged, non-committal. Some heads were shaken, but privately, as though unintentionally, the head-shaker thumping the table with the rest, but not so as to make the glasses rattle.

'A toast, ladies and gentlemen.' The portly chairman stood up. 'A united Ireland!' That they could respond to. Grizelda sat, and absently received the congratulations of her neighbours, none of whom she thought quite up to the mark. The real struggle was taking place elsewhere. None of the new men was here.

Not far away Brian MacDermott sat in a small sitting-room, shabby, without ornaments or pictures, tied to a kitchen chair. In the kitchen was taking place what Finbar called a Revolutionary Tribunal. Outside only an occasional car passed. The evening rush was over. The town was settling down.

Within a few moments Finbar would emerge and shoot him. Brian felt sick and tried to compose himself. He tried to think that, after all, this was the fate he had planned for Finbar, but the thought gave him no comfort. Then — he took in his breath with a sob that he tried to choke back — he heard the scrape of chairs in the kitchen and Finbar, with two others Brian had hardly seen before, came into the room holding an automatic with a silencer on it. His face was scored red with gashes from the barbed-wire he had dived through, and his hands were bandaged, each finger separately. He is going to be able to pull the trigger himself, thought Brian.

'The Tribunal has sentenced you to death,' said Finbar.

'You have no authority,' said Brian, his mouth dry, his voice humiliatingly strange.

'We are taking it. From you and the rest.'

'What is the charge?'

'Betraying me, Colm, Henry and Sean.'

Brian tried, without moving his eyes from Finbar's face, to say his prayers: 'Hail Mary, full of Grace . . . and at the hour of our death, Amen.' He asked forgiveness for his sins; he was sorry, truly sorry, for all the meannesses in his life.

Finbar was talking: '. . . stood in the way of the progressive element. Politically we must move forward. You are a man of the past who will not move. We have no choice.'

'You are a fool,' said Brian, to keep him talking.

Finbar began again, speaking of his political intentions. Brian thought sickly of Jamesy, of their times together. But sickly only at first. Almost at once a warmth began to infuse him, a warmth that was like a light also. He saw that his feeling for Jamesy was the best part of himself, was all, perhaps, that mattered, his pure feeling. He saw that it was love — not love for Jamesy particularly, though Jamesy was the focus of that love — but love that was like a part of God's love for the world, he understood that now, love that was indistinguishable from perfect simplicity, a huge energising force that ruled the earth and the stars. Finbar moved his gun up.

It was warmth and light and a picture. Very simple, as though this simplicity had lain hidden at the bottom of his soul, buried under complexities he had not guessed, for he had thought of himself as a simple man. But, ah, not, not with the simplicity he glimpsed now. The picture was of the sea, the sun rising at the edge of it, inexorable, red, a cuticle, a semi-cicle growing more yellow, flooding the world with warmth and light, that could not be prevented — God! He could not go now! not now, when he saw so much and it was so simple! The light flooded the whole of space, white, and there was a roaring too, as though of millions of wings.

'Jesus!' said one of the men. 'He died smiling!'

'What a bloody mess,' said the other.

Finbar stood, looking at the slumped figure. 'He was a good man.'

'*Was* right enough!' One of them laughed. Finbar's eyes rested on him.

'He was a good man in a fight, for the Cause.'

'He was that, Finbar.'

'And I had to do it.'

'No choice.'

'Clean up the mess. Stick a label on him putting it down to the Prots and leave him where I said.'

'Leave it to us, Finbar.'

There was a pause. None of them moved.

'I'll get the actor soon,' said Finbar, wearily.

'What about the young feller?'

'What young feller?'

104

'Jamesy. He was the one who grassed. Not Brian.'

Finbar turned slowly, the gun still in his hand. 'You never told me that.'

The man's mouth fell open. 'I thought you knew!'

Finbar turned back to Brian, and contemplated him. 'It makes no difference,' he said, after a moment. 'I'll deal with the kid later.'

An old woman stood in the narrow hallway. She was bent, dressed in a black shawl. 'God bless you, son,' she said, without raising her head. 'God bless you.'

Finbar forced himself to touch her, he knew it was expected, and laid his fingers on her bony arm, like a blessing.

She placed her own hand over his and he shivered slightly, it was as though she wanted to touch death. Then she opened the front door and looked both ways along the street. 'Go your ways,' she said, as Finbar stepped past her, 'and may God love you all your days.' Walking away he heard her still muttering blessings as she shut the door. He turned up his collar. The evening was cold.

8

'*Hawk with ruffled feathers on the Bow-sprit — Now shot at & yet did not move — how fatigued — a third time it made a gyre, a short circuit & returned again (5 times it was thus shot at, left the vessel, flew to another and I heard firing, now here, now there and nobody shot it but probably it perished from fatigue & the attempt to rest upon the wave! — Poor Hawk! O strange lust of Murder in Man! — It is not cruelty, it is mere non-feeling from non-thinking.*'

The events of the last few days had tired Dougal. He dozed a little and then turned the pages of Coleridge as he lay, dressed, on his bed. Lust of murder.... Had that fellow MacDermott actually *killed* people? He'd been quick enough to cool down the young one, thank God.

Lara was on the other bed, telephone on her stomach, receiver stuck between hunched shoulder and ear. Americans always seemed very at ease with telephones.

'We can have the house!' she said to him, in the way people have when they are listening to somebody else on the line.

'Oh,' said Dougal.

'What's that, Bully?' She waved her hand at him to keep quiet but he had nothing more to say. 'Sorry, Bully, the line's bad. You sound as though you're talking through a grapefruit. Maybe you are!' She giggled; she seemed very happy. 'What? No — a *grapefruit* ... Oh forget it, Bully, start again. What was that about a plane?' She covered the mouthpiece with her chin. 'We may have to do a movie for Bully. He's being kind and there's bound to be a bill. Yes? Yes, Bully, I'm still here.'

Dougal rolled off the bed and wandered to the window, still carrying the Coleridge, his finger marking the place. In the harbour terns were fighting for fish-guts that floated in

the water, going 'tippy-tippy-*tin*' as they quarrelled, like
the refrain of that old song. The main ferry went past, the
Saint Olaf long and white, its lit-up portholes glowing
yellow in the dusk. He turned back to the room to compare
it with the portrait of its predecessor that hung on the wall
and immediately his eyes rested on the picture it fell to the
floor and its glass smashed.

'Stop knocking the furniture about. Bully's on the line to
his London office, he'll be back to me any minute. He's had
this terrific idea . . . Yes, Bully? What? Oh *come on*! Who's
the writer? *Alvin*? You can't be serious! Now Bully, anyone
would think you're trying to obligate me. Well O.K., O.K.,
we'll talk about it later, but what did the London office
say? They *did*? How soon?. . . Bully, you're a potentate,
you're a king. . . .'

Dougal was superstitious. It could not have been the
wind that blew the picture off its hook because the window
was shut and anyway, for once, there was no wind. The nail
must have loosened itself in the plaster. But he couldn't
help wondering if at that moment something dreadful had
happened somewhere, something to do with him. Or was
going to happen . . .

He lay on his bed again and thought how right poets
were to go on about things like terns, to make you look at a
world outside the human. Watching them he had found
himself breathing easier. He should read more poetry.

'Philosophy to a few, Religion with many, is the Friend of Poetry;
as producing the 2 conditions of pleasure for poetry, namely,
tranquility & the attachment of the affections to generalisations. God,
Soul, Heaven, the Gospel, miracles &c are themselves a sort of poetry,
compared with Lombard St. and 'Change Alley speculations.'

His father had lived by generalisations – Honour, Cour-
tesy. Of course they were poetry! The words still thrilled
Dougal, if he let them. Grizelda lived by them too — the
Nation, the Cause. But to Dougal these were "'Change
Alley speculations" — and murder.

Lara was still crooning into the telephone. The call was
going to cost all of the twenty-five quid he had given the
manager.

She put the receiver back in its cradle, the telephone back between their beds and stretched herself flat, triumphant.

'I've done it!'

'What?'

'Got us out of here. There'll be a plane waiting for us in an hour. He got hold of a pal, an oil chief, who keeps one up here in case he wants to visit an oil-rig.'

'But we don't want to visit an oil-rig!'

'*Funny* Dougal . . . His pilot'll fly us to Surrey. We'll be there before those writers get back from the island. It's a jet.'

'Wow!'

'Baby did it!'

'Bully did it.'

'You don't sound pleased.'

'Of course I am. Marvellous. Well done.'

'I may have to do a film for him — he strikes bargains.' She looked across at Dougal. 'I'm sure he'll want you too.'

Dougal surprised himself by his annoyance. '*That* doesn't matter!'

'No. . . . Anyway, we're saved!'

What Dougal said next made him curse. It had seemed the mere truth as he spoke, but as soon as the words were out he knew they were unforgiveable. 'I'd be just as content here, really.'

'Oh *Christ*!' She was really angry, jumped on the floor to rage at him, standing at the foot of his bed. 'I've been playing the whore with that Bully for half-an-hour. A pig who propositioned me on the set when I was thirteen. I play the bastard along so we can be together, start again, in England. And all you say is "Ai'd rawther be heah, ectually!" '

'Sorry, Lara. I wasn't thinking — it was reading Coleridge.'

'*Fuck* Coleridge!'

She snatched the book from his hands and flung it at the wall. Following its path Dougal saw she had no shoes on.

'Mind the broken glass.'

She looked down, still raging, and checked her step. Then she threw herself into a chair, red-faced, and stared out of the window.

This is entirely my fault, thought Dougal. How far from Grace I almost permanently am.

He could not resist looking down too, at the Coleridge that had bounced from the wall onto the floor by his bed. He leaned over guiltily, and read, as a kind of *sortes Vergilianae*: '*Do not be too much discouraged if any vertue be mixed in your consciousness with affectation and imperfect sincerity, or some vanity — disapprove of this — and continue the practice & the good feeling even thus mixed — it will gradually purify itself.*'

There was a knock at the door. Getting off the bed, in his socks, he opened it. A girl peered past him at Lara, at the broken glass. 'The manager would like to see you about the call.'

'Yes, of course. I'll come down now.' Shutting the door, putting on his shoes and jacket, he said. 'I'm sorry, Lara. Daft thing to say. I'll love Surrey.'

'You'll hate it!'

'Not with you I won't. As you say. We'll start again. It'll be fun.'

He reached for the dried-out crumpled notes in his pocket and smiled at her, putting all he could into the smile.

It will gradually purify itself . . .

Not long later William Binkley, in London on a flying visit, was interviewing Michael Merry in the bar of the Royal Court Hotel. He sat in silence, brooding, staring at Michael, who stared back. A young assistant, expensively and casually dressed, sat at his side.

'Alvin Karoff is working on the script right now,' said Binkley, at last.

'He's good,' said Michael, taking the opportunity to reach for his drink, and sip, thinking that as one grew older the humiliations attendant on one's profession did not diminish.

'We got Lara Gray.'

'I thought she'd retired. She's certainly gone into hiding somewhere.'

Binkley grunted. 'You'll like the part. Strong.'

Years before Michael might have thought that meant he was cast. Now he knew it meant nothing. It certainly did not mean he would like the part.

'Dougal Kerr's reading it now.'

Michael, unblinking, returned the producer's stare. Did this old toad think he could out-act an *actor*? 'I thought he'd gone into hiding too,' he said, widening his eyes.

'I hid them both.' Binkley permitted himself a smirk, at which the young man laughed.

'They're friends of mine,' said Michael.

'We'll be in touch,' said Binkley.

Immediately the assistant was on his feet, tenderly propelling Michael towards the door. 'We have your agent's number. I *do* hope it all works out.'

Outside in Sloane Square Michael Merry blinked at its green, crouched statue and experienced the keenest temptation of his life. He knew where Dougal Kerr was . . . and there would be others, in Ireland, who would like to know that.

The papers had been full of Dougal and his heroism. Only Dougal could acquire heroic status by running away. . . . As he stepped through Eaton Square, bound for the Garrick, he thought that if he teased Dougal about that publicity he would pretend to know nothing about it. What a crook the man was.

Dougal was arranging small pebbles along the edge of William Binkley's drive. They were smooth and nearly round — from Chesil Beach probably — and he liked bending to pick them off the grass and the feel of them in his hand. Too many large cars, approaching the splendid portico too fast (or leaving it fast, fleeing from Binkley) had squirted them with their tyres from the edge onto the grass. They had been annoying Dougal for days.

He liked the bending because he was pleased at the continuing elasticity of his spine and because be believed it did his waistline good. His life in Virginia Water, with Lara, was disagreeably sedentary. The swimming-pool was bunged-up — or so the sulky servants said. There seemed nowhere to walk, or only past municipal-looking trees behind which houses like this one were hidden, or along empty roads past bus-stops in front of litter-bestrewn scrub, the kind in which women's murdered bodies were found. It was a rotten, slightly sinister place to hide. If that's what they were doing.

It was lonely, too. They read, Lara cooked small meals (rather well). She had forced Binkley's staff — two men and a girl, all of dauntingly upper-class mien — back into their palatial 'Staff Cottage', where they sulked. When the two of them were together in the evening they watched television and drank slightly too much. If only her great Public knew how dull Lara's life was! . . . *I'm* all right, thought Dougal, except for being in this ghastly place, and that can't go on forever — but what about Lara?

He placed three grey pebbles in a line so that their convexities and concavities nearly interlocked and realised that he had addressed that question to his father.

He straightened up and stood, absently watching a couple of wagtails on the drive. The image of his father persisted. How he had loved the *theatrical* nature of his father's life! Probably why he had become an actor, though the Old Man had hardly entered a theatre in his life. With their rods and guns and pipes his father and his friends had insisted that life was as they wished it to be and they created it anew every day in the form they desired. He did not do that.

Dougal had expected that kind of adulthood to come with age but it had not. He was not grown-up as his father had been. He created no world. Nor was he the source of comfort and assurance to anyone, not in the way his father had been to him.

Dropping the stone he held, making the wagtails startle, he began to wander through the house. It wasn't bad,

Binkley must have found someone good to do it for him. But it was a stage-set for something that wasn't happening. The servants were stage-hands, demoralised by inaction. Thinking of which . . .

'*Books are dear companions but*' — what was it he'd said? That he often wanted to talk with the author? '*At times I become restless: for my nature is very social.*' Just so . . .

Lara was out, conferring with Binkley in London – the screen-play was awful. Might be fun to go up there himself, on his own, bump into a few people, have a drink. Might even pick up a pointer to some decent work. Anything would be better than poncing about in Binkley's movie.

He left the house and walked to the cottage which stood apart; school of Lutyens, not much smaller than the main house. He pulled the hanging bell. A young man came to the door, his arm deep inside a riding-boot, which he continued to polish, raising his eyebrows at Dougal. Surely Binkley didn't *ride*? Impossible. This chap probably did. To hounds.

'I'm going up to London, Tom. Lara's out. Will you lock up?'

'O.K.'

'Have you the keys of the Porsche?'

He half-feared the chap would say that he was using it himself, and wondered what he could say in return, but he vanished and returned with the keys which he held high, dangling them in his fingers, dropping them from a height into Dougal's palm.

'Thanks. Back tonight. No need to prepare supper.'

The man smiled, said nothing. Walking away Dougal thought irritably that his father would have got to know that chap and would have handled him better.

He enjoyed the drive to town, in a reasonable amount of sunshine, feeling youthful in the beautiful car.

In London he parked the Porsche near the Duke of York steps and standing beside it, locking up, suddenly wondered what he was going to do now; half-wished he belonged to the Athenaeum opposite, so that he could scuttle inside. He had never belonged to anything. But he felt too old to be alone.

He found himself in Trafalgar Square, which he had always disliked, the place seemed inimical to good weather; something to do with the architecture. In St Martin's Lane he stopped outside the Albery and was shocked to see they were doing *Private Lives*. Not *again*! Good part, though. . . . Well, good-*ish*. He went into the Salisbury, which he had always liked, it was like being inside a cut-glass jug.

An unkempt, pale young man stood next to him at the bar. Dougal recognised him as an actor whose work he admired.

'Hello.'

'Hi,' said the young man, unsmiling.

'We haven't met. I'm Dougal Kerr.'

'I know,' said the young man.

'I liked *Checkers*. You were good.'

'Thanks.'

For a moment Dougal thought he was going to say no more but then he went on, looking round as he spoke, never looking at Dougal.

'You've been doing some improvising for the Provos.'

'Yes.' Dougal had been careful to read none of the newspaper accounts, from embarrassment. He understood Abraham had laid it on a little. He had read however of Brian MacDermott's mysterious death; had been saddened by it, with an odd sense of having lost a protector. It was not a subject he wanted to talk about.

'They still after you?'

'I doubt it. They've got better things to do by now. Or worse. What about you? What are you up to?'

The young man looked into his glass as though he saw something floating in it. He said he was part of a group forming an actors' co-operative, converting an old church in a suburb.

'I'd like to do something for you,' said Dougal.

For the first time the young man showed some expression, which might have been dismay.

'I don't think we're doing your sort of stuff.'

'Good. I don't want to do my sort of stuff. I'd like to play a tramp, or a drunk, or a homosexual, or all three at once.'

'Yer "cameo",' said the young man.

'O.K. Or a lead. If one's going.'

'Slumming?'

'I'd like a change.'

'Ah.'

'I'd like *to* change.'

'What makes you think we're doing plays about tramps and homosexuals?'

'I don't know what the hell you're doing. Shakespeare? If you're mixed up in it, that's good enough for me.'

The young man continued to look about him, uneasily, as though for escape. Dougal watched him with amusement.

'Yeah. See you.' With that he disappeared, leaving Dougal standing alone at the bar. For all Dougal knew 'Yeah. See you' meant he had gone to discuss Dougal's employment, with his colleagues, or to laugh at him. It didn't matter. The graceless laconicisms of the time didn't matter either. He looked at his reflection in the glass behind the bar, barbered, tailored. . . . He felt no need to change that. He had become, imperceptibly, a creature from another age. So be it.

Then his heart, like a boy's heart, lurched. He saw in the mirror, behind him, sitting at the table with a young man, *Elizabeth.* He knew the way that hair fell, those shoulders slightly stooped, in a way that he did not quite *know* anything else. And could that young man be Jim? How terrible not to be certain whether it was his own son, that slice of his secret, inner life . . .

He was tempted to run but was transfixed, looking at his wife, his first wife, ex-wife, but he could not think of her like that. She was smiling at something the young man was saying — he seemed very attentive, bent towards her — then, with a slight duck of her chin she looked vaguely round, their eyes met in the mirror and Dougal, after a moment, turned.

Was her smile different now that she saw him? Dougal could detect no difference, neither increased warmth nor any loss of it. She was more self-possessed than he was, he realised, with a stab of loneliness.

He approached them and the young man stood up. Dougal saw with relief that it was not Jim — he would be

115

seeing him soon anyway, and on his own — and he was much too young for Elizabeth.

'I half-wondered if you'd be here,' she said, looking up at him. 'I remembered you sometimes used to come here.'

'May I join you?'

'Philip, this is Dougal Kerr, Jim's father.'

'I know. How do you do?' The boy continued to stand, awkward. He had been enjoying himself with Elizabeth and now he did not know what to do.

Dougal resisted the impulse to put him at his ease, said nothing and seated himself on the unpolished bench opposite Elizabeth, staring at her.

'I discovered Philip had never seen *Private Lives*.' She half-giggled. 'I couldn't resist. . . . Have you ever played Elyot, Dougal?'

She had seen him play it. It had been his first success, just after they were married.

'Yes,' he said.

She looked grave, staring back at him, nodding, half-admitting her mistake, trying to concentrate, so that she would not say anything else like that.

Dougal glanced up at the young man, still standing, and raised his eyebrows at him, smiling.

'Philip.' Elizabeth sounded decisive, motherly. 'I forgot. I ordered the tickets by telephone. One is supposed to collect them at the box-office half an hour before. I *wonder*. . . . would you be so sweet? And it would give me a chance to say hello to Dougal.'

The boy went off, mumbling farewells, bumping into things.

'Half an hour,' said Dougal, when he had gone.

'Well, twenty-five minutes.'

'I miss you all the time, Liz.'

She laughed. 'You've become very famous. A hero, too.'

'I wasn't much good as Elyot.'

'I remember it well. I can't think why I said that. Startled, I suppose. Saying the first thing that came into my head. Philip is Jim's closest friend . . .'

'We haven't long, Liz.' He stared at her. She fiddled with

116

her gloves, on the table in front of her. Her hands were slightly redder, more knobbled, than he remembered them. Housework? She looked prosperous: A Chanel suit of fawn, with dark brown trimming along the edges, a blue silk blouse; she looked delicious. He thought: I know every mannerism. And it isn't that I just remember them. When I first saw them they were familiar, as though I remembered them then . . .

'We're moving to Norfolk,' she said.

'Very flat, Norfolk,' he answered, absently.

'Yes, but the light's marvellous.'

I was never any good in that damned play, he thought. Didn't believe in it. If those two idiots were so keen on each other, why had they ever parted? Elizabeth hadn't remembered. It had been his first West End role. He'd been playing it ever since . . .

'I can't remember why we parted,' he said.

She gave a gasp. 'Dougal, it's all so long ago.'

'Is it? I don't think things like that exist inside time at all. They're outside it.' They are, they *are*, he said to himself, bewildered. He did not know whether it was pain he felt, being with her. He felt at home, but lost at the same time. Almost hysterical. 'I can't just let you go like this. What would you say if I swept you up, bore you away and we lived happily ever after?'

She was equal to this, pretended he was teasing, though she must have seen that he was in some sort of earnest. 'And leave that poor boy waiting forlornly in the foyer, the bells going, everyone going to their seats?' She looked at him.

'So that's what you'd say.'

'Yes.'

'I wondered.'

The worst of it was she seemed *fond* of him, it was like a barrier. 'You see — everything you do; the way you touched your gloves just now, the way you move your chin, is different *in kind* from the way other people do those things! It touches some part of me that nothing else does, nothing else that happens around me, I mean. It's not just that I love you. Though it's that too, I suppose. It's somehow more than that. Did you ever feel for me, in that way?'

'Dougal — '

'Because if you didn't, I don't think you should have married me.'

At last she showed distress. But it was distress for *him*, he saw that.

'Oh Dougal, we do so many things we shouldn't do. Sometimes quite innocently.'

So. He digested this. She had never felt for him in that odd, infinitely special way. The way that apparently lasted till the grave. Maybe beyond the grave.... He had guessed it of course but never quite admitted it to himself. Now he had to. It was the last nail going in. It did not exactly hurt. It entered some long-dulled place his being had curled itself protectively around, maybe to ache later. Yet all he felt now was a purely selfish gratitude that he could still respond to the physical being, the uniqueness, of anyone, as he did to that of Elizabeth.

He began quietly, absurdly, to sing, looking at her, overbearing her embarrassment.

> 'Someday I'll find you,
> Moonlight behind you,
> True to the dream I am dreaming.

Except that it isn't a dream, the feeling I have. You'll be hearing that song in a minute.'

'I know. I knew about Norfolk, too. You must come to stay.'

'Oh . . .' He raised his hand despairingly, letting it fall. '*Elizabeth*!'

'But it all seems so silly. . . . There are peope who *never* feel the way you do, the way you say you feel about me. I don't think I've ever felt like that. For anyone.'

It was a crumb she gave him. He seized it, but it was flavourless. She went on:

'When I realised that I — well, that I couldn't give you what you expected of me — '

'Was I so demanding?'

She hesitated: not consciously demanding, but oh yes demanding! Now he was looking at her, intent, as though much depended on her answer. 'Not really,' she said. 'No, it wasn't that. It was just that I felt that one day you'd realise it wasn't quite the same for me and you'd be hurt. Things would go sour, *I* would go sour, hurting you, and I felt I had to stop, before it was too late. I suppose I mean before it was too late for me. Maybe.' Her voice trailed away, as though appalled at the vision of herself.

'You were strong.'

'Hard, you mean?'

'No.'

'Oh, you don't know what it's like leaving someone!' She hesitated again, and said uncertainly. 'Do you?' When Dougal made no reply she went on, in a rush: 'And there was Jimmy, of course. He's all right. You've been marvellous. But I felt terrible, for years. I've never *been* left. Not yet, anyway. But sometimes I've felt it *must* be worse to be the leaver. But you were so easy, in so many ways. You found life so easy. I felt you must be all right. In the end. Were you very hurt?'

'More surprised, I think. At first.'

She clapped her hands. 'You see?'

I really *have* got her going, thought Dougal. That was relief, exaggerated. She's been moved. So. '*Easy*' Dougal. . . . He'd thought that the best way. And he had lost what he most wanted.

'I must go, I really must.' She stood up, gathered her gloves, her bag, with the slight clumsiness he remembered, unlike the deft precision of an actress. She was flushed, she had forgotten to push her hair from her face. Now she frowned slightly, very serious, looking away. 'Perhaps what you say you feel for me, darling Dougal, is a gift. Perhaps it doesn't go with possessing at all, not necessarily. Is like a sort of vision, that you have to take with you through life?'

'*Second* prize?'

'Oh, I was a cow. I had to be.' She still looked away. 'I don't know . . .'

'No, you weren't.' Although there was time left Dougal found himself helping her towards the swing door; she seemed flustered, lost.

She stood on the pavement outside, looking anxiously up at him, her hair blown across her face. Dougal knew she wanted him to forgive her, and he did. But he was not going to say so. He felt desolate.

'You haven't changed,' she said. 'You seem so soft — in a good way. So soft and easy. But there's something inside you that's adamantine.'

'Bad?'

'Not a bit. But I don't like actors. I like you but I don't like actors.'

'Are they so different?'

'Maybe not. But I think so. I think I prefer — ordinary people.'

'You said that before. Years ago.'

'You couldn't find anyone more ordinary than Bill.'

A tiny bit of disloyalty, to please him? Too late to know. He still had an image of hailing a taxi, hauling her inside: '*Drive anywhere, fast!*'. . . But there was something inside her, too, that he came up against. At the same time he had a sense of their two beings mingled, as flames mingle. It had been intended. He was sure he had not been deceived.

'And Lara?' she asked.

'No. Lara is not ordinary.'

'Look after her, Dougal. *Oh*,' she gathered her bottom lip in her teeth, '*don't* look like that! Is that the worst thing I could say? There was no hurt in what I meant!' She stared down at the pavement, looked up. 'Well . . .'

He took her hand and cupped the palm of it round his cheek, feeling, as he did so, even more physically warmed, than he had expected.

She disengaged herself, turned and walked away, fumbling in her bag, peering down into it. What for? Dougal asked himself. Tickets? They were with the boy. She had to do something because she was disturbed. He must not disturb her again. For the moment he could think of no reason why he should ever do anything else.

'Care for a drink?' A voice from behind made him turn. It was the pale young actor, who now seemed to be re-entering the pub. 'No thanks.' Dougal continued to stare down the street. Elizabeth had gone.

'Please yourself.' The actor continued to stand there, almost menacing.

'What?' *Good Lord*! Perhaps he *had* been off to discuss a part for me, with his mates. Dougal ran his hand over his face. 'All right. Just bumped into an old friend.' He continued to mumble as they entered the pub. 'Unexpected — rather startling.'

The young man regarded him coolly. 'It happens.' He jerked his head interrogatively at the bar.

'An enormous Scotch,' said Dougal.

After the smallest of hesitations the actor ordered a double, and half a pint of Scotch Ale for himself. He was not an actor for nothing; the pause told Dougal that large Scotches were Shaftesbury Avenue, were 'showbiz'. Then he began to talk, in a monotone that was strange in a man whom Dougal had seen rise to musical eloquence on the stage, about a project he, or rather 'they', had in mind: a communal enterprise. 'Easy'? thought Dougal. Am I 'easy'? The play, or 'project' or whatever it was, as the young man droned on, his eyes now never leaving Dougal's face, sounded gloomy, as well as not easy.

9

'When you draw nearer
You'll smile an little smile —
In a little while
We will stand
Hand in hand'

Not this side of the grave we won't. After that — on the other side — Dougal was prepared to believe anything. He certainly found it impossible to think that the feeling he had for Elizabeth would just end, with death. Because although it was as particular as possible, it seemed an oddly *impersonal* feeling, as though drawn from some secret vat the world contained; a dole from the world-ladle, given, and then the vat shut. Elizabeth had been quite right, it did seem like a gift.

He was standing, quietly singing, in a small snug, almost cubby-hole, in a pub in Chesham Place. He was known there and, drunker than he knew, he had felt the need to gather his thoughts.

It had been a long day.

Turning his drink in his hand he looked round him at the panelled walls. Years before, between marriages, he had had a flat nearby — it was at the height of his notoriety, the studios had been trying to turn him into some sort of British Gregory Peck. He could hardly go anywhere without being accosted, stared at, flirted with, propositioned, or punched. Odd how little he had minded. Thought it part of the job.

He was alone. The rather dwarfish landlord's wife had

locked the street door on the inside when she recognised him. Probably thought he was still being hounded.

For the second time that day he caught sight of himself in a mirror. Damn pub mirrors! What on earth were they there for, anyway? He did not like what he saw. Too light-weight, too Peter Pan. Too 'easy'. . . .

He became conscious of someone leaning over the bar in the Saloon, trying to get a better look at him, round the corner. He took a step backward and sat down on the narrow wooden settle, more suddenly than he had intended.

The young actor had taken him to meet a group of others. First buying a half-bottle of whisky in the pub; probably he imagined Dougal could not function without it.

During the course of the afternoon Dougal, obedient, shy, and thinking of Elizabeth, had drunk it. The writer of the new play had been there and they had all discussed his script. Dougal's suggested part was that of a hitherto successful actor who had turned against his profession (which seemed fair enough), who drank, didn't wash, stole, cheated, and spent much of his time eloquently inveighing against 'society'. So did the other characters. It seemed to Dougal they would have been unpleasant slags in any set-up, but perhaps that was the author's point. He wasn't sure. Dougal had never thought much about 'society' at all. Just taken the pickings, he supposed.

He remembered that he still had the script under his arm. He reached forward for his whisky from the bar — bending his knees so that he would not be spotted from the saloon — and began to read it.

It was a mess all right, by *Private Lives* standards. Almost impossible to stage, needed a huge cast. They were to be six people in a disused church. But the dialogue was good, better than good. Ordinary speech, slightly heightened, with a different rhythm for each character; the scenes had rhythm, too. Dougal became quite excited, as he read.

He glanced ahead quickly, to one of his own long speeches. God! He had to fart, belch, fiddle with his fly-buttons, threaten to expose himself. . . . Strewth! His heart quailed, but at the same instant he decided he would do it, do all that was required of him. Do it properly — or rather, *im*properly . . . he giggled into his glass.

Must be careful. Tight. Long drive in a minute. To *Surrey* . . .

The problem was — to become grown-up! He freely admitted that he wasn't 'grown-up.' Who was?

Fuzzled, over-tired, he addressed himself to the question as an actor approaches a new part. Whom could he model himself on? What mannerisms, shoes, clothes, would help him into the adult role? And then perhaps *become* it. Coleridge had said that any good pretence would 'purify itself'; and presumably leave behind the real thing.

The only person who fitted the bill was his father.

What was 'grown-up' about him? Answer: that he, as a consequence of a disastrous marriage to Grizelda – she was always going on about 'society' too, come to think of it! — had become entirely, unbitterly, unillusioned. Tired-looking but good-humoured; without self-pity. That chap MacDermott had been unillusioned too.

Dougal — asking for, and receiving, another conspiratorial whisky — took account of his own illusions. He had recently abandoned two. The first was that he had discovered he could send two men to their deaths (in 'self-defence') without a qualm; at least at the time.

And today he had confirmed (what he had known for years) that the woman he loved did not love him. No, it was worse than that. He had confirmed that she failed to love him not because he had faults, or neglected her, or anything like that. He just did not inspire in her the feelings she inspired in him.

Then why the bloody hell had she married him?

No self-pity. That's not in the 'grown-up' part.

(This damned play isn't grown-up, either. But it's sincere, and clever-*ish*. — Might be the first step towards *me* growing up? Off, off, you lendings. Hah!)

. . . But there was something much more important, about Father.

125

Yes!

Unillusioned, he had discreetly, almost unnoticeably, devoted a good part of his life to ensuring the welfare of another person. (Not for 'society' — though he may have done his bit, for all Dougal knew.) For another, identifiable, flawed, *ungrateful* human being.) Me.

I've never done that. For anyone.

Jim's different. I've always got on with Jim. Not as a Dad, though. We're mates. I think we are.

Unsteadily, Dougal stood up and found himself face to face in the mirror. Unconsciously he tried to look grave, senatorial. Unrewarded care of another. That would have to be for Lara. . . . He thought it almost with surprise. Duty. Perfectly clear. 'Purify itself'. Become the real thing, maybe. But that doesn't matter.

He took a five-pound note from his pocket and, scrawling on it. 'Bless you, darling. Dougal' he left it on the bar under his whisky glass. Next time he'd probably find it hanging up, framed. . . . Ah, vanity! But he had rather enjoyed them, the vanity years.

He unlocked the door and let himself out. On the pavement he tried to remember where he had left the car. Remembering, making his way towards it, the extra attention he had to pay to his balance endowed his walk — fortunate Dougal — with a new gravity and weightiness.

At the Duke of York's Steps he stared down at the shining Porsche, trying to remember how he came to be driving it. When it came back to him he laughed nervously; he had drunk far too much. However, it was long before closing-time, there wouldn't be too many policemen about, on the look-out for drunken, fledgling grown-ups.

He reached their part of wooded Surrey in safety and, as he drove under the orange street-lighting, along the empty wide roads, he thought how much he loathed it. Within every carefully invisible house, hidden at the end of its excluding tree-lined drive, there slavered, he felt sure, a man-eating Dobermann-Pinscher.

He left the car at the top of his own drive and let himself into the dark house. At least no dog, thank God.

126

He was surprised to find a light in the drawing-room which at first he thought was empty. Then he saw that Lara was asleep, stretched full-length on the sofa, glass on the floor by her side. He had a moment's anxiousness, but she'd been pretty good of late. Almost housewifely in fact, and anyone would pass out after a day of Binkley.

The room was panelled in bleached oak, with recesses containing vast flower-arrangements, consisting of hot-house irises, which always filled Dougal with gloom and the air with a heavy, sickly odour.

He pressed one of the panels and it swung open, revealing a refrigerator stuffed with every kind of liquor, daily re-stocked. He poured himself a drink; difficult to stop, once you've started. He took it over to one of the enormous armchairs, which almost enveloped him, opposite the proportionately huge, low-backed, red-and-black sofa on which Lara slept.

First he contemplated the room, then he contemplated his wife.

Oak-panelling, vast flowers too symmetrically arranged, concealed drinks cabinet absurdly over-filled — it was exactly the sort of place people would expect someone like Lara to live. Courtesy of Bully. Just as his ghastly, mean-souled films were the ones people expected Lara to be in. The distant Bully reached out, and controlled, and diminished.

Lara's small shoes were neatly side by side on the hearth-rug. She was very disciplined in some ways, brought up in a hard, loveless school. Her stockings were twisted, her hair damp against her cheeks, her mouth slightly open. He looked at her with affection. Her ridiculous life was what he had tried to rescue her from. It had been O.K. at first. She hadn't been able to have kids. An abortion had messed up her insides apparently. Then she began to slide a little. More than a little . . .

He had been away a lot at the time. Each time he came back she seemed worse, so that he was relieved to go away again. He probably should have stayed with her but there began to be a kind of awe in him, at her willed disin-

127

tegration. It was as though she was on a journey to the bottom, and he had somehow felt it impious to interfere. He was glad, at least, that he had never had the cheek to tell her to pull herself together. Although . . . maybe she had wanted him to.

Now she was back more or less where he found her. With Bully. A bished-up rescue attempt if ever there was one. But she seemed better.

She stirred slightly, and gave a little whimper. It was probably the whisky but Dougal really felt that perhaps he could bring her some of that ladleful from the vat which Elizabeth had given him — or, at least, had been the cause of his receiving. Whatever it was. But good stuff, crystalline. Otherwise it would be wasted . . .

His eyes on her woke her up, and she smiled sleepily, with pleasure at the sight of him, which moved Dougal.

'Hi, honey. You been there long?' She sat up, yawning. Dougal watched her becoming more guarded, like a cat. It was always like that. But he remembered her first smile. 'Where the heck d'you get to?'

'The place seemed pretty empty. So I went to London.'

He looks damned happy, she thought. 'Meet anyone?'

'Not really . . . Oh yes. I bumped into Don Hart.'

'Who?'

'You know, the young actor. We saw him in *Crackers*.'

'Oh, *him*!' she said, grumpily.

'How was Bully?'

She yawned again. 'He agreed to all the script changes. *All*.'

'Marvellous.'

'What's that you're drinking?'

'Whisky.'

'Hey! this *is* a party! I've never seen you with such a dark one.'

Dougal held up his glass and examined it, blinking. 'Must be a dark sort of whisky.'

'Can I have one?'

She watched him carefully as, back to her, he pressed the panel.

'That means no locations.'

'Oh good,' he said pouring the drink. He brought it over and, while she arranged the cushions behind herself, not taking her eyes off him, she said as though to a child: '*No locations*. That means it's all *studio*. We could stay here. We're so *near* the studios.'

Dougal looked at her. Her eyes were anxious. 'Couldn't be better,' he said.

'But you detest this place!'

'Not a bit,' said Dougal, looking round. 'It's fine. I love it.' At that moment he did. Strange things were happening tonight. But she had looked so nervous . . .

'Do you *really*, darling?' Lara sounded genuinely astonished, and grateful.

'Of *course*.'

'I just don't want you going back to that awful Ireland yet, or being chased over bogs. I just don't *want* that! I want you safe. It's safe here.'

'No bogs. Promise.'

'Will you take the part?'

'What part?'

She was patient again, talking to a child. 'The one Bully wants you for, Dougal. In his *movie*. Remember?'

'Um — no.'

'The character *is* a dumb-bell,' said Lara. Having gained her main point she was willing to concede this one. 'You could make something of it, though,' she said, unconvincingly.

'Don Hart has offered me something else.'

'That actor who drove me crazy?'

'I thought you liked him in the part.'

'He was fantastic! I couldn't *stand* him! He played a horrible little man and was so horrible I wanted to spit in his eye!'

'So?'

'That's not how it's done . . . Did I ever tell you about *Come Back Little Sheba*. You know it? The lead is a boring woman. This damned director wanted me to *be* boring. That was his idea of theatrical "reality". Boring the audience.'

'I didn't know you did *Come Back Little Sheba*?'

'I didn't. I spat in his eye. Where are you going to do this — slice of reality?'

Dougal told her.

'*Where*?'

'You 'eard.'

She was silent for a moment, staring at him. 'Why do I ever let you out of my *sight*!'

'Can't think.' He stood over her, smiling. 'It'll be fine. You coining millions from Bully — *for* Bully — '

'I get three percent of the gross.'

'You *did* have a good day! And me, after a hard day harrowing the pews — I wonder if they'll take out the pulpit — coming back to a candle-lit supper, just you and me and the moonlight, among the tall, sighing *safe* trees of Surrey. And so to bed.'

'It sounds marvellous,' she said, quietly.

'You've got to believe it.' He knelt beside the sofa and slipped his hands under her shoulder-blades. Her long arms linked, a tentative triangle, behind his neck. He kissed her, feeling her mouth unprepared, unresponsive.

'*Dougal*!' The astonishment in her small cry told him more than, at the moment, he wished to think about.

'You know, Lara — I think I'm a little tight.'

'What fun,' she said quietly, her arms tightening round his neck.

Jamesy concentrated on the wires inside the old man's transistor. His hands shook. One word too many and the old fellow might clam up.

'Oh, yes,' the old man was saying, 'a terrible business right enough,' his eyes watering; anxious to be off with his radio.

'I'll need to do a bit of soldering here. Won't take long.' Jamesy stood. 'But the Prots never claimed responsibility.'

'Maybe he was mugged,' said the old man, scratching his chin. 'Terrible violent this town is.'

Jamesy went to plug in his soldering iron, pushing past the knees of the old man as he moved to the wall. 'Shot in the head,' he said, his back to the old man, trying to keep his voice steady. 'By a *mugger*?'

'Well, a bad business, that's for sure,' said the old man, with an air of closing the matter. 'A fine man, your uncle, Jamesy. One of the old Brigade.'

'And Finbar's in charge now?'

'You could say so. Have you not done with that thing?'

'This is micro-electronics, Mr Keogh, not easy. Would Uncle Brian have liked Finbar in charge?'

'He would *not*.' The old man slapped his knee, petulant. 'He wants us old ones out. Not a word of thanks for all we've done and the way we paid for it in English dungeons. He'll not give you the time of day, that man!'

Jamesy stuck out the tip of his tongue as he carefully pressed the wire into place. 'Would you tell me if Finbar ever plans to go to London? Please?'

'What's that?' The old man was indignant. 'Why should I do such a thing! What's it to you? Wasn't it you that blabbed in the first place and brought all the trouble on your poor Uncle?'

Jamesy went very still. 'So it was Finbar killed him!'

The old man began to shout, terrified. 'I never said that! God forgive you! You've no call to be putting words in my mouth! Here, give that over to me!' and he grabbed the transistor from Jamesy.

'Try it,' the boy said.

The old man stared at him, muttering. Then, out of curiosity, he pressed the switch. A race-commentary gabbled out and an expression of bliss covered his face. 'That'll be the 2.15 at Leopardstown. I've a bit on the 4 o'clock.' He now looked shifty. 'Will you be wanting payment now? I'm a bit short just at the moment. Tonight, now, after the race?'

'Just tell me if Finbar ever plans to go to England. Will you? Where's the harm in it?'

'Where's the harm?' said the old man, doubtful.

'I've a score to settle there.'

'You have so?' He looked shrewd. 'And what's that to do with Finbar?'

131

'Well, in England they'd be looking for him, wouldn't they? They wouldn't bother about me.'

After a pause the old man slapped his knee again. 'You're not Brian's nephew for nothing, Jamesy — God rest his soul!'

'Jamesy?' His mother called up the stairs.

'Just coming Mrs O'Hanlon,' called back Keogh. At the door he winked. 'You're a right one! Do a little job when all the rozzers are combing the place for Finbar. . . . You should be in the Unit. I've always said so.' He winked again and laid a finger to his nose. 'I'll put in a word.'

'Wait till I've done the job.' said Jamesy, dully.

His mother stood in the doorway, looking from one to the other. The old man pushed past her, chuckling, the radio under his arm.

When she heard the front door slam she said: 'What's between you and that old skite?'

'I was fixing his set. He risked his life, years ago.'

'Did he?' She sounded unimpressed. 'All he fights now is a bottle of stout.'

'You've changed, Mam.'

'Hasn't everything?' She went to his window and looked out of it. 'Will you mind the young one for me? I've to do the messages.'

'I will,' said Jamesy.

'If you could get a job, now, mending your wirelesses and things, that'd take your mind off. You'd think there was enough people wanting those things mended!'

'There's enough mending them already. I went to Murphy's this morning. No vacancies. They said try England.'

'Did they so? Maybe that's not a bad notion.'

'You *have* changed.'

She stared at him. He'd be safe in England. . . . 'Did you get any money out of your man?'

'I did not.'

'Oh, Jamesy. . . . He's a useless old fellow, never out of the betting shop, never giving his wife two bob to rub together. *I* could use a bob or two, you know.'

132

'He promised tonight. When his horse comes in.'

'That'll be the day!' His mother was silent for a moment, then she laughed and said: 'Poor old soul! I'll only be a few minutes,' and she was gone.

Jamesy listened to her steps in the hall, heard the front door slam, and remained where he was. She often forgot something and came back for it.

After what he judged was a sufficient time he knelt and reached under his bed, lifting one of the bare boards, pushing his arm over the joists up to the shoulder. His fingers touched the butt of Brian's gun. He withdrew his arm, satisfied, replaced the board and sat on he edge of his bed.

A noise came from downstairs. Something, or someone, had fallen off a table. There was the beginnings of a wail.

'Oohooo, Shay. I'm coming. What have you done now?' and he ran downstairs.

Michael Merry was taking tea with Grizelda in her first-floor drawing room.

He had a week out of the film, which was now well under way, and had half-consciously been drawn back to Dublin, sniffing the air for anything that could satisfy what he recognised as his increasing obsession with Dougal. He had hoped that Lara might invite him back to Binkley's Surrey house, but she had not.

He had telephoned Grizelda on the off-chance, hoping to hear of Dougal, and now, in her high drawing room, it did appear that she wanted to talk of him. In fact he thought he detected in her a store of malice that shocked and delighted him. The old boy, he thought, did rather seem to inspire it.

They sat facing each other, tea-cups balanced.

She was saying: 'Is it not rather expensive to stop a film in mid-career, as it were? All those technicians, and so on?'

'It is not the film that has stopped. It is I. For a week.' Michael smiled modestly.

'You have a small role?' said Grizelda, negotiating the corner of a small sandwich with the corner of her mouth. False teeth, thought Michael.

He said: 'To small for Dougal, certainly.'

'He was offered the part, before you, and refused?'

'So he told me, when we met.' A *white* lie, thought Michael. They had not met. But I want to see what she will say.

'How unusually unkind of him. . . . He's always so very *sweet* to people. So dislikes unpleasantness. At least, that is my impression.'

'Dislikes it very much. Marvellously easy chap to get along with.'

'Nevertheless, unpleasant for you, to think you are picking up his left-overs — but then, you are great friends.'

'We have known each other for twenty-five years.' He saw her black eyes glitter in her white, powdered face.

'I suppose,' she said, 'that amounts to the same thing.'

'You must be very close to him.'

'Not at all,' she said, with a certain sharpness. 'He is not an easy person to get close to. I daresay you have found that.'

'He rather *lurks*, doesn't he. Stands slightly to one side, I mean. Doesn't belong to any clubs or anything. It can be rather disconcerting.'

'Dear Dougal. He has charm, but I doubt his capacity for deep feeling.'

'Perhaps so.'

'Then he picked up with that glamour girl they used to rave about.'

'She was marvellously beautiful. Still is, on her day. I'm working with her now.'

'Always drunk when I met her. Dougal's fault, I suppose.'

Michael Merry, putting a twinkle into his expression, decided to take a risk. 'I don't think he gave her enough,' he hesitated — 'of what she wanted.'

Grizelda gave a surprisingly bawdy laugh, like a quack. 'Did she want much?'

Michael Merry giggled with relief: 'I dare say.'

'Can't say I blame Dougal there. She stank like a fox.'

'Oh, she's much better now.'

'Really?' She sounded disappointed. 'Dougal always seems to come well out of things.'

'He does seem to land on his feet, certainly.'

'You find that an endearing quality?'

Michael made a face. 'One is only human.'

Grizelda smiled. 'That business on the island. He was extraordinarily lucky in that.'

'You must have been so relieved.'

'Of course.' She levered herself up and, with her arms on the mantel, her back to him, she gently rearranged some small coals on the fire with her toe. 'I've often wondered how they were so quickly on his track.'

'I'm afraid I'm rather guilty there. I let something slip. I had no idea, of course. . . . As soon as I got word of it I went to the island at once.'

'To help Dougal?'

'Of course. But he'd talked his way out of it by then.'

She was silent for a moment, her head bent over the fire. 'You know why he passed that information to the authorities? To hurt me. I sometimes think he hates me.' She sounded matter-of-fact.

'Oh, surely not!' said Michael, enjoying himself beyond measure.

She turned. 'Do you think they're still after him?'

'For giving away the information? I doubt it, don't you?'

'The man who chased him was shot.'

'Odd, that.' If either of them had any thoughts on the matter they did not voice them. There was a silence, broken gently by Grizelda.

'I don't even know where he is.'

'Hiding away, rather. At least he was. Now he's in a really terrible play. In the suburbs.'

'His career is not going well?'

'The play was panned.'

She stared at him. 'You rather like that, don't you?'

He met her eyes. 'I do, quite.'

135

She gave one of her surprising deep laughs. 'And you know where he lives.'

'Yes, he's —'

She held up her hand. 'Don't tell me!'

'But surely *you* wouldn't — .' His smile was forced. He wanted her to know.

'I don't like being two-faced with my comrades. They might ask me where he was living.' She stared at Michael. 'You don't like him much, do you?'

'I can't get him out of my mind.'

'I can,' she said, seating herself again. 'Do have some more tea.'

'Deirdre! Is Jamesy home?'

The first floor window went up. 'What's all that noise you're making, Mr Keogh?'

'There was no answer to the bell. It's my TV set. It's gone all wavey. And Jamesy fixed it last time.'

'He told me it was nearly done for, that set. You'd been kicking it.'

'I was wondering if he'd just have a look. It's the races.'

'He can't.'

'What d'you mean "he can't"! What sort of a job is that, to fix a set and it blows up at once!'

'Did you pay him?'

'I did so. I gave him what he wanted.'

Deirdre stared down at the old man. 'What does that mean?' she said.

'I can't be shouting all night, out in the street. Will he come or won't he?' The old man was petulant. 'Where is he?'

'In England.'

'Ah,' said the old man. 'Ah.'

'What?'

'Nothing. I'll not be bothering you, then. You haven't,' he said as an after-thought, 'you haven't a couple of bob on you, have you? Just till tomorrow?'

Deirdre hesitated. 'Oh' — she reached down into her bag and threw him a coin. 'There! Buy yourself a new set with it!'

'God bless, Deirdre. And God rest your brother Brian. He was a good man.'

Deirdre stared after him, and then she slowly let down the window.

What had the old idiot meant by 'what he wanted'? He was still thick with the fellows — though Brian had had little time for him. Surely 'what he wanted' could have nothing to do with that? Not after Brian. . . . She stared ahead of her, thinking. Jamesy had said there was a job in England. A 'job'. . .

She had come into his room straight from the street. She missed him and wanted to be alone to think about him. Now she went down on her knees by the side of his bed to pray that it was a repair-man job he was after in England, not any other kind. Something caught her eye below the bed. She looked under it and saw the dislodged floor-board, not quite replaced. She moved it and revealed the hiding place. It was empty, as she had known it would be.

'Mary, mother of God!' she said into her hands, beginning to cry. She had had enough of that.

10

Every night — and even more so every *matineé* — Dougal could feel the audience's disappointment, and their growing dislike.

He built a wall between himself and them and, on stage, opened himself fully for his fellow-actors: the only piece of the world that existed for him, during those two and a half hours, was the lighted platform on which he and his colleagues moved and spoke.

It was the first time in his career that he had done this, and he found it exciting.

He did not blame the audience, most of whom had come to see him. Some of the other actors were well-known, some were even good, but his was the name that brought in people who did not normally go to the theatre at all. At first he had felt a kindly need to reassure them, to show them that the Dougal Kerr they wanted was still there, was only pretending to be this embarrassing man. But as time passed the temptation to do this grew less, and then it faded altogether. He forgot the audience.

He liked the people he worked with well enough. They took the play and themelves a shade seriously, as though they thought they were telling the audience something it had not known before. Whereas Dougal believed it was no part of an actor's job to deliver a message, all he had to do was to make the part he was playing believable. He certainly missed the light-hearted cynicism of the theatre he was used to, but this was more interesting. He had been more bored than he realised.

Lara observed the change in him. In a way she feared it. She had always known Dougal would never be anything but a second-rate film actor because there was a part of himself he would not give, it was as though he winked at the audience, and past the camera lens. It was this detached amusement that she loved. She had been surrounded by blood-givers all her life and they became vampires in their turn, monsters of need. A Dougal who was a *good* actor, with the psychic disruption that seemed to entail, would be no good to her.

But he was more attentive these days, which was nice. Except when he was doing it on purpose, which made her savage.

As far as Dougal was concerned things seemed to be going pretty well. True, he and Lara saw little of each other — she was at the studio all day, he at the theatre in the evening, and often she was driven to work before he awoke. But she seemed in good form and his resolution to look after her was, on the whole, easy to keep. This business of 'taking pleasure in Duty' — so that it ceases to be a 'duty' at all, but fun — seemed to work well. Coleridge had got it right. He thought less of Elizabeth and more of the part of himself that the feeling for her had opened up; instead of protecting it, like a pocket of sweetness, inviolable, he tried to let it spread to other bits of himself, like grace. So it sometimes seemed, anyway. But she astonished him when she turned on him, wolfish. He couldn't make that out.

He sometimes remembered the way Brian MacDermott had looked at Lara, when they met at Mrs Strachan's. It had been a speculative, *religious* look, that Dougal puzzled over. He found, as he thought of MacDermott, an increasing interest in him.

Dougal did not know what MacDermott, with his mystical sense of Ireland, had known at once: that Lara was a Muse, exigent, unforgiving. Dougal's complacent self-congratulations would have amused him. Brian would have known that Dougal's public and private lives were beginning — at last — to come together; or, as he would have put it, become politicised, no wasting gap between the private and the public man. Dougal's actor's performance of the devoted husband, like his performance in the theatre, could only work when he forgot his audience — and himself. Anything less, any self-regard, was punished by the Muse, who made no concessions and, being a goddess, need have no idea she was any such thing. This was the way MacDermott thought of Ireland, and it gave him what strength he had.

One night Dougal was pleased to find Lara still awake, sitting up in their bed going through a pile of cuttings sent her by the studio. He fixed himself some supper, a cold leg of chicken, a glass of Meursault, and took it up to eat it with her in the bedroom. She was still picking through the cuttings, shifting them about, not reading them.

'Anything interesting?' He knew there wouldn't be. He had never seen her looking at them before.

'There is one thing.' She took one from the pile with no hesitation, she had obviously been waiting with it. She held out Michael Merry's interview with an Irish paper. Dougal stood up, collected it, sat down again and read, gnawing the chicken bone.

'What of it?'

'That's an Irish paper.'

He glanced at it. 'So it is.'

'They'll know where we are.'

'Mm? They could have found out ages ago if they'd wanted to.'

'Yes, but now it's in print. They're politicians. They may have to do something to save their faces. Why the hell did Michael have to talk like that!'

She felt, rather than saw, Dougal go still. 'He told them about the cottage, didn't he? That's why he was on the island that day, to see what had happened?'

'He's a funny guy . . .'

'Jesus *Christ*! He wants you *dead*!'

'Oh, come on.'

'Let's get a dog!'

He laughed. 'They'd only chloroform it. Lara, they don't want *me*. They're too busy blowing up other people.'

'They followed you to the island.'

'To show their long arm, etcetera.'

'You never read what they said about you in the papers, did you?'

'No.'

'They made a *fool* of that man MacDermott. A stupid bog-man outwitted by smooth Dougal Kerr. When he really let you off!'

'I know he did.'

'When he got back they shot him. For being made a fool of.'

'We don't *know* that.'

'What would you do, Dougal, after you'd shot a man for being made a fool of, cared enough about bad publicity to shoot him? Would there be any loose ends, d'you think, you might want to tidy up? To make the point?

He took a sip of wine. 'I do see what you mean.' The Meursault, opened yesterday, was a bit sharp. He had not made a fool of Brian. He was not responsible for his death. . . . 'Dread of the ludicrous while a great man is talking to me with a holy passion.' Oh *no*! He had not meant. . . . Was there nothing he could touch which did not go horrible. He smiled again. 'I'll get you a dog if you want one. A ravening brute. Trained to eat Irishmen.'

'Don't smile like that, Dougal. You look like a death's head!'

'I liked MacDermott. I thought Michael Merry was a friend.' He said it quietly.

He began to pad round the room, taking off his clothes. He hung up his jacket in one of Binkley's cupboards, big as dressing-rooms, picked tomorrow's checked shirt from a drawer marked with a white plaque WHITE SHIRTS. He put his coloured shirts there on purpose, Bully's plaques annoyed him so much.

'You mustn't worry about the future, old gel. You know the mortgage on this house is in your name. The servants will look after you, dear old souls, been in the family for years. When they come in from riding, that is, or driving the Porsche. I'll even leave you the dog. Such faithful companions! Tell you what! You can go and live with my mother!'

142

To his relief he heard Lara's gasp turn, almost, into a chuckle, as he switched out the light and climbed into bed beside her.

'I am frightened,' she said in the dark, lacing her fingers with his under the bedclothes.

'Don't be.' He was serious. 'Nothing of that kind's going to happen to me. I feel it in my bones.'

'I like the feel of your bones.'

'I know how those people think. I'm the son of one of them. Remember?'

'My God, how could I forget!'

'Well, they've forgotten about me.'

For a long time afterwards he lay awake, confessing to himself that he had no idea how their minds worked. But mostly he thought of Michael. What in God's name had he ever done to Michael?

Lara had worried him, despite himself. He had always thought that Binkley's part of Surrey was suited to a murder. It was all bushes and trees and empty roads — a place where it always seemed to be Sunday. The vegetation was of the evergreen kind — laurels, Scotch pines — that he detested near towns and it made him long for the bright wet greens of Ireland. Coming home at night he found himself inspecting any lone walker he passed in his car, and before getting out of it he had caught himself more than once peering into the bushes opposite his own front door, with his engine still running, prepared to make a break for it if anyone emerged.

On the whole these things made him feel foolish. Lara had infected him. She would not have been so scared of her own, native, Mafia. It was the unknown that got her down. To her these Irish-English feuds were as mysterious and as creepy as the warfare between Chinese Tongs.

He did not buy her a dog because he knew more about dogs than she did. It would have to be trained, exercised, fed. A puppy would not have been much use, and anything else — was it possible to buy a fully-trained guard dog?

unpleasant thought! — would probably have terrorised *them*.

It was a Sunday evening. They had spent a restful, yawning day together. In the morning Dougal had even taken Lara to Mass and she had surprised him with her attentiveness. She was always surprising him.

It was late, they were sitting by the fire. Outside it was raining softly. Lara had been reading a Fay Weldon with small exclamations of irritation. Now she was eating scrambled eggs on her knee, a second supper. Dougal had refused some for himself. She certainly seemed to pack in vast quantities of food. Yet she was as slim as ever.

He was reading, as usual, Coleridge; or rather, re-reading, dipping into him, breaking off to watch Lara. After a wink at her when she caught his eye in mid-chew – to which she did not respond, deep in her own thoughts — he went back to him. He was going on about duty or, as he spelled it, 'Duty'. This was good stuff but there were pages of nothing-very-much round it as though Coleridge was scribbling to kid himself — or others? — that he was working. Or from 'Duty'? hoping the writing would purify itself, become the real thing?

'*Humanly happy I call him who in enjoyment **finds** his Duty . . .*'

Dougal stared above Lara's bent, scrambled-eggs imbibing, head. He had of late, and at last, been trying to do his Duty towards her and found it enjoyable. She was lovable. Presumably he had always loved her or he wouldn't have married her; he couldn't remember and didn't try. But it seemed there were something like love-muscles that expanded with practice, as your thorax was supposed to if you used a chest expander.

'*Do not quarrel too harshly with your present self: for all virtue subsists in and by Pleasure.*'

He felt pleasure: was comfortable. Probably he was, at the moment, smug. But he did not feel inclined to quarrel too harshly with his present self.

He frowned: '*The hot-blooded Paddy's **pruriency** for a fight.*' Possibly true, but why 'Paddy'? Why did the English invariably patronise the Irish, who were more articulate, in many ways more subtle? It was racial. Imagination-envy, easygoingness-envy . . .

But he frowned deeper; was trying to remember something about Duty that had shocked him; something English and cruel. He turned back a few pages and found he had marked the place with the burnt end of a match, by an exclamation mark:

'I would not willingly kill even a flower, but were I at the head of an army, or a revolutionary Kingdom, I would do **my duty** *and tho' it should be the ordering of the military execution of a city, yet — supposing it my Duty — I would give the order, & then in awe listen to the uproar, even as to a thunder-storm the awe as tranquil, the submission to the inevitable, to the Unconnected with my own Self, as profound. It should be as if the lightening of Heaven passed along my Sword, & destroyed a man —* '

Of all the thousands of entries, that was the first that seemed to him nonsense. It begged so many questions! Why should C. merely have to give the order and then be permitted to listen, 'in awe'? Why shouldn't he have to kill people himself? Children — there would presumbly be a few around? What he said was the madness of the world, and here was marvellous, intelligent, *human* Coleridge saying it! Dougal put down the book dismayed, wondering whether there was some aspect of human behaviour that he failed to understand. He noticed Lara staring past him, fork raised to her mouth.

'Get up!' said a voice.

He turned, and with the serendipity that had more than once accompanied his reading of Coleridge, found himself staring down the barrel of a gun.

How had this man got in? He must have been amazingly quiet! There was the noise of the rain outside, the fire-noise . . .

'Up!'

He was wearing one of those extraordinary balaclava things with slits in it. Did they draw them from the QM Stores. . . . *One mask, Woollen, Freedom Fighter, for the use of* . . .

'Against the wall. Right against it.'

145

Dougal felt the wall behind him with his palms. Pressed his back hard against it.

The man raised the gun, holding it at arm's length, pointing it at his head.

'We execute you in the name of Ireland for the death of Brian MacDermott — '

'I had nothing to do with it!'

'For passing informtion to the enemy — '

'Not *my* enemies!' Keep talking, keep talking! . . .

'And because we find it expedient.'

The man settled his feet apart, gripped his right wrist with his left hand and tightened his grip on the gun. Lara, who had been sitting perfectly still on the sofa now launched herself at the man in a clatter of plate and cutlery, a slither of scrambled eggs, and clutched at the man's ankles: 'No! Leave him! Shoot me! Please!' Her hands clawed up his legs, twisting themselves in his trousers, her face cleansed, purified by the intensity of her pleading.

Dougal, looking at her face, was astonished. She means it! he thought. She really *loves* me. . . . Why should she do that?

The man tried to push her away with his leg but she clung on. Dougal wished she would not. It seemed likely she might panic him into getting it over with before he lost his balance. But he pulled his foot free and shoved her away with it, towards the sofa. But it was a surprisingly gentle shove . . . then Dougal understood: he would not harm her because he knew who she was! He would not harm her because she was Lara Gray. A great wash of relief made him almost light-headed for a moment but the gun levelled again, steadied — 'the lightening of Heaven passed along my Sword' — then a bang, glass breaking, and the man went over, his gun bouncing on the rug.

'I killed him! I killed him! I've a sin on my soul!'

It was Jamesy.

'How many of you are there, for God's sake?' croaked Dougal.

'I killed him! He killed Brian. God forgive me! He came on his own. He's mad.'

146

Lara was on the floor, huddled against the sofa where the man had pushed her.

'Oh Christ!' she kept saying. 'Oh Christ! Oh Christ!'

'I've a sin —'

'No you haven't!' said Dougal, gasping. 'Was he really alone.' The words came out of him like steam escaping from a kettle, he could speak only in short spurts. 'Get him out of here. You too. Help pick him up.' The dead man was lying on a Persian rug. 'Take these two corners.'

The boy did not move. 'Yes, he hated you, for mockery.' Dougal picked up the corners and held them for the boy, who bent and took them. 'Lara. Back the car to the front door. Open the boot.'

She stared at him for a moment, then she rose quickly and went out. 'Do nothing if anyone's about! Warn us,' called Dougal. Thank God he'd left the Citroën near, and it had a big boot. The servants' house was distant. They usually had Wagner on full blast. . . . 'Right. Up he comes!' He was unbelievably heavy. The boy let one of his corners slip, and the man bumped on the floor, lop-sided. 'We'll drag him.' Dougal picked up the fallen gun and put it in his pocket. Together they pulled him over the parquet into the hall.

The car was backed-up to the door, boot open. With a huge effort, Lara helping, they heaved the body, on the rug, into the boot. Dougal had a moment of terror as they did so, that his back would go. What then? It didn't. They shoved the bewildered boy into the back seat and Lara took the wheel.

'Where to?' she asked quietly.

'That disused quarry a few miles down the road. Thank God it's raining!'

'What do we do if anybody stops us?'

'Why should they?'

For a while Lara concentrated on driving. Then she said: 'Why are we doing this?'

Dougal touched her knee, drawing her attention, and pointed with his thumb to the silent boy in the back. 'That's one reason. The other is — if they knew we were connected with it . . .'

'You think it might all be over now?'

'Sure. If this works. Thanks, by the way.'

'What for?'

'Oh. . . .' He remembered her face, pleading. 'For not saying "I told you so".'

'I'd have gotten round to it.'

At the quarry, the rain now pelting down, they heaved the man out, slithering and slipping, and somehow got him behind a bush. Dougal pulled the rug from under him and body jerked limply.

'Oh, God,' said Lara.

'Could they trace a thing like this? Better take it back. Burn it. Bit of a mess.' Dougal held it gingerly in one hand. It was muddy, and there were other things on it. He threw it in the boot. He took the gun from his pocket. 'Can I have your scarf?'

He cleaned the gun and dropped it by the man. 'Give me yours,' he said to the boy. 'Can it be traced to you?'

Jamesy shook his head, his hair in streaks down his face, his teeth chattering, looking as he had done on the island. 'It's Brian's. I took it from him. The day he . . . ,' and he began to cry.

'Brave lad, brave lad,' Dougal muttered reluctantly, bundling him back into the car. The gun he hurled as far as he could into the undergrowth of the quarry.

'You somewhere to stay?' he asked, as he drove off.

'Yes.'

'I shouldn't go back to Ireland for a bit. They might put two and two . . .'

'Only an old man knows anything. He'd be too frightened to talk. And they know Finbar was mad.'

'You thought it out well.'

'It was for my uncle. I'm loyal still.'

'Of course.' Dougal could not look at him, and spoke fast. 'Need a job?'

'I have one.'

Dougal drew up near a small station. 'Trains run till midnight. Out quick. Shouldn't be seen together. Money?' The boy nodded. Then he left the car, and walked towards

148

the distant lights of the station. Dougal drove off at once. After a while he drew to the side and stopped.

Sitting in the driving-seat, staring in front of him, he drew what seemed the first breath since he had stared down the barrel of the gun. Then he breathed out noisily, slumping back, closing his eyes.

Lara shyly, almost unbelievingly, ran the tips of her fingers down his cheek.

'That apalling *mask*,' she whispered, awe-struck.

'Their sisters knit them.'

'Why do they *do* it?'

'Knit?'

'Follow people?. . . Kill them?'

'Spoil your scrambled-eggs?'

'*Why*?'

He could find no relief, slumped back; it was still as though he could not breathe. He feared he might pass out, He opened his eyes wide and, leaning forward, put his forehead on the coldness of the steering-wheel.

' "Duty",' he said, and began to wind down the window in case he was sick.

EPILOGUE

Norman was painting Drusilla, in his cottage on the island. He had not been there for over a year. Mary had married a man in a tinned-food company — Norman and she had not parted on good terms — and anyway, the cottage itself, after the publicity given to the exploits of Dougal, had for a while become a place of pilgrimage for trippers.

However, it was four miles from the ferry, the ferries themselves were infrequent and the seas hostile, so the early enthusiasm of sightseers had faded, as had the memory of the Dougal story. As had Dougal himself, apparently; Norman had heard of his mania for taking unsuitable parts in worthy, non-commercial plays. Norman, as he stared at Drusilla, trying to concentrate on his canvas, thought of Dougal in this room, remembered his irritating Richard Hannay-like assurance, and the way Mary had looked at him. Well, he was on the skids now. Some people take life too easy, probably owed his career to Lara Gray anyway. Apparently they were still together (he'd read somewhere) but it was unlikely that a woman like her would stay forever with a man who had grown so dim.

He even owed Drusilla's presence here to Dougal, damn it. . . . She was writing a book about the 'Irish Problem' — or so she claimed — and had accepted Norman's invitation to come and view the scene of one of the more recent incidents, and to meet that old blether Abraham Muir.

Norman was not particularly interested in figure-painting, but getting Drusilla out of her clothes seemed a step in the right direction. She had been reluctant, he had pressed the point, and now she lay awkwardly in front of

151

him, because of the size of the room, only a couple of feet away, and his hand shook. It was also unbearably hot. He had boarded-up the windows — so that by Tilly-lamp he could get an even light was his explanation, but he had hopes of the extra privacy the boards afforded — and she had asked for a paraffin-heater so that she should not be cold. With the lamp and the stove and the boarded windows the room was like Kew; he desperately wanted to take off his own clothes and was waiting for a moment when he might dare suggest it.

'You are very beautiful,' he said hoarsely, squinting along his brush which, held at arm's length, was an inch or two from her flesh.

She stared at him with large eyes. She was so *young* — a new generation! He had no idea whether she expected him to pounce or would startle if he did. . . . How did one *ever* know? He would have to make a move soon. Streams of sweat were running down the inside of his polo-necked jersey.

'Would you mind if ?. . .' He began to pull the jersey over his head, noticing, before he disappeared inside it, that her eyes showed no change of expression when he did so. It was noisy inside the jersey and in mid-pull he stopped and held his breath. It *couldn't* be . . .

It was. He had heard voices. Good God Almighty! Might as well have a cottage on Stephen's Green and be done with it! There was a knock on the front door.

'Damn! Damn! *Damn*!' he said, reappearing, pulling his jersey down again. 'Stay there! That's perfect! Don't move! I'll get rid of them.'

He went to the front door and opened it a crack. Then he opened it some more and released the knob letting it fall open wide, like his mouth, as he stood there, beyond speech.

In front of him stood Michael Merry and, beyond him in the rain, was *Dougal Kerr*. 'Bloody hell,' he said at last, flatly, as though winded.

Merry, hearing a noise from the side room, extended his neck and saw Drusilla standing, naked.

'Oh, I'm so sorry,' he said, not stepping back. 'You're *working*. . . . It was just that I prevailed on Dougal to show me some of his old haunts, we happened to be passing here, and —'

'Dougal? Does that mean Dougal *Kerr*?' Drusilla sounded excited.

'It is he. And *I* am Michael Merry. . . . How do you do?' He stepped back at last, making room for Dougal to pass him. 'There's someone in there seems to know you.'

Dougal looked surprised, automatically stepped forward and saw Drusilla at the end of the box-bed, now with the corner of a blanket held to her breast, her flanks bare.

'Dougal Kerr!' she cried. 'I'm writing a book. Can I interview you?'

'Look we really are most frightfully busy. It's a tricky part of the painting I've reached. Mind coming back in a couple of hours?'

'Of course,' said Dougal stepping quickly into the rain.

'Of course,' said Michael, smiling, retreating more slowly. So slowly that he was left smiling at the shut door.

Inside the cottage Norman turned to face Drusilla. She looked like a bit of Victorian prurience, by Etty, or Alma-Tadema; half-draped, utterly inviting. In his desperation he was conscious of licking his lips.

'*Dougal Kerr!*' she said, like a schoolgirl. 'Look, if you want to have it off, for Chrissake get on with it!' and dropping the blanket she padded back into the room.

Norman stood still, dumb-founded, utterly dismayed. 'No,' he found himself saying. 'It wasn't that . . . I mean . . .'

'O.K.' He heard her rustling into her clothes. 'For God's sake get those bloody boards off the windows! I'm boiling!'

Oh damn and blast to hell Dougal Kerr . . .

It had been Lara's idea that they should come up to this place, and invite Michael. She had been curiously insistent. Dougal sensed that she wanted to rub his nose in the full extent of Michael's 'treachery', make him see

153

things as they really were, instead of as he wished them to be. Dougal did not feel he needed lessons in reality from Lara. Anymore than he needed to read bad novels stuffed with horrors in order to understand the 'world'. However, she had wanted this trip, and he wanted to please her.

Once they were within range of the island, installed in a mainland hotel, an odd threesome, Michael had seemed eager to cross on the ferry to view the location of Dougal's 'triumph'. 'It was, after all, rather an *epic*,' he said.

Lara could not face the crossing, memories of her previous ones were still too vivid, so the two men, Dougal acquiescent, increasingly curious about Michael, had crossed without her.

There seemed some kind of pressure inside Michael Merry, a sense of something coming to the boil, and Dougal patiently waited. If there was to be a showdown it would not be of his making.

They were now standing on the headland by the deserted village, where Jamesy and Brian had sheltered from the wind, and shared Deirdre's sandwiches.

The rain had briefly stopped, the green sea sparkled, so did the grass and the wet stones of the ruined houses. For once there was not too much wind. Dougal was watching the head of a seal that had disappeared in the swell and then emerged again, to watch them. He was thinking two things: what fun it must be for the seal living in two worlds, the smooth green chambers where it was so sleekly at home, and the strange upper air of coloured cliffs and jagged rocks and two figures standing, looking down. He was also thinking of Brian MacDermott: that he was dead.

He bent to pick up a couple of round stones, cast up to the top of the cliff by some huge wave.

Michael was asking him about his future plans. 'I saw you in the last one you did.'

'Did you?'

There was a long pause. Dougal expected him to say no more.

'You were good.'

Dougal was surprised. Michael would tell the truth

154

about such a matter. Yes, he had not been too bad. He had hopes of becoming an actor, one day . . .

'I stayed with Elizabeth and Billy a while back.' He glanced sideways at Dougal. 'I didn't like to mention her in front of Lara.' He paused again. Dougal said nothing, watching the seal. It had gone again, a sudden absence in the swelling sea. 'She talked of you. Was quite forthcoming. . . . I think she's a trace bored with her old William.'

He had given up his little jerking glances and was now turned, looking at Dougal, frankly examining his reaction.

Dougal had none. He swung his arm, underhand, and one of the stones plopped into the sea. He half-expected the seal to dive for it like a dog, so domesticated it seemed. Yet it was entirely wild, and content.

'Shall we go back?' He realised he was indifferent to whatever Michael Merry thought or did — and always had been. Yet he had thought that was friendship! No wonder the man hated him. How had he ever become so careless of other people? However — 'do not quarrel too harshly with your present self' — or your past self. 'All virtue subsists in and by pleasure'. It was a pleasure to watch the seal. He did not know why. Had MacDermott seen it?

He had been brushed by violence but still did not understand it. Perhaps it was important to understand it. If he pushed Michael off the cliff, would he understand it then? He weighed the stone in his hand: bash in his head? He had a feeling Michael would almost like it. Might wish to be relieved of some kind of demon he contained. Maybe that *was* violence, that wish to be relieved of some demonic pressure? But MacDermott did not seem to have a demon . . .

'Do you ever think of the man who was after you here? The one who was shot in Dublin?'

'Sometimes.'

'You were lucky to get away with it twice.'

'Twice?'

'The one they found dead in the quarry. Near you. It must have been you he was after.'

155

'D'you think so?'

'They found Lara's scarf near him.'

'Yes.'

'How the hell'd he get that?'

'Recce'd the house, d'you think, took a souvenir? I don't know. Probably a fan of Lara's.'

'What did the police think?'

'They were puzzled. Asked a few questions. I couldn't help them. They seemed relieved the man was dead. Apparently quite a big fish, escaped from gaol.'

'One of the men you had put away.'

'The policeman kept on saying, "bloody murderer". I tried to explain.'

'Explain what, exactly?'

That he wasn't a murderer in his own eyes. He was a politician. Question of angle. Much easier for him *not* to be a gun-man. He'd still be alive, apart from anything. So would MacDermott. The cop didn't seem to understand.'

'You were asking a lot.'

'Mm? I don't think the English ever do understand.'

'You don't think of yourself as English?'

'Not really.'

'For years you were everyone's idea of the perfect Englishman.'

' "Was". Now it's over to you.'

'Yes.' He sounded pleased. 'You don't mind?'

Dougal tried to think of an answer that would give pleasure. 'A bit.'

'Bully was furious with you about that rug.'

'I sent him a cheque.' About the last of my spare cash, he thought.

'Said it was priceless.'

'It got burnt.'

'Yes, but he wanted to see it, in case it could be mended. "Where *is* the goddam thing" he kept saying. How'd it get burnt?'

'Log out of the fire.'

Michael nodded. 'Not carnage in the old homestead? Blood on the carpet, and so on?'

Michael made good guesses. Malice is very per-cipient.

'No.'

'Anyway, he aint 'alf got it in for *you*. Tells everyone you stole his Azerbaijan, or whatever it was. Lara just laughs. We both tease him about it. Still — it could be awkward for you one day.'

Was he having an affair with Lara? Anything is possible, and Dougal told himself he ought not to mind. He knew he was becoming a bore. Well, he always had been a bore but when he was successful it showed less. Nowadays he seemed not to care how he appeared to others, or to himself. . . . Lara is loyal and good but I can't expect her to stick to a broke and boring me. Not her style. God I pat-ronised her, as well as Michael! Thinking I could help. . . .

'I've a new flat in Dublin. You'll never guess where! In your mother's house. . . . She had all that space. We get along rather well.'

Moving into every corner of his life, triumphant. But they were always corners he had left, to be alone in.

'Shall we go?' said Dougal again.

'Back to Norman?'

'Strewth, no!'

'No.' He sounded disappointed.

Dougal suddenly had the idea of putting his arm round Michael's shoulders; he did so, awkwardly, and saw a succession of expressions cross Michael's face: aston-ishment, mistrust, hope. Good God! *The man wants us to be friends*! Has done for years and it seems to have driven him mad! Dougal tightened his arm, appalled.

'Dear old Michael. . . . But we'd better push on. Lara has her first drink about this time. She's been off it for a bit. Waiting for us she might forget and have too many.'

'Poor Dougal,' said Merry. '*Good* Dougal.'

'Only by mistake,' Dougal said, and led the way back along the valley. Then he realised he might have been misunderstood and turned, waiting for Michael to catch him up. 'I mean Lara's mistake. About the drink. Us being late.'

When they neared the hollow stone, walking in silence, Abraham appeared, lurking as usual near his favourite place, the genius of it. He was dressed as he always was: old belted raincoat, porkpie hat, town shoes.

They stopped and talked, Michael fidgeting, Abraham asking when Dougal was coming to live on the island and bring his beautiful wife. 'When the wind drops,' Dougal said and Abraham silently acknowledged the pawkiness of that. 'You've the makings of an islander,' he said.

After a while they parted, Abraham wandered on, probably to sit smoking and looking down on the broken walls of his birthplace, and Dougal was once more oppressed by the sense of tension in Michael at his side. He let his thoughts wander round Abraham, whom he liked, and who had nearly caused his death because of his fondness for a good story. He thought of Betty Corrigal and her lonely sky-swept grave, of the German's head falling from the sky, and of the seal in the sea.

'That fellow seemed to regard you as some sort of tourist attraction!'

They had reached the jetty, and disturbed a flock of black and white oyster-catchers that flew off low along the shore with small cries.

'Once maybe,' said Dougal. 'Not any more.'

'I wonder,' said Michael, unable to keep the bitterness out of his voice. Dougal watched the ferry approaching, a small point on the heaving sea.